About the Author

Elizabeth Uywin was born in Braintree to a farming family in 1951. Most of her childhood memories are of helping her father on the farm, until her family moved to London to be near her grandmother.

She worked as a secretary to the chief news editor of the Press Association and in the court service for many years. Elizabeth Uywin is widowed and lives in Godstone, England.

This is her fourth book. She previously wrote the trilogy *Voices from the Past*.

This book is dedicated my three daughters, who never fail to surround me with love.

Elizabeth Uywin

THE POISONED PEN

AUSTIN MACAULEY PUBLISHERS™

LONDON · CAMBRIDGE · NEW YORK · SHARJAH

A CIP catalogue record for this title is available from the British Library.

ISBN 9781398442054 (Paperback)
ISBN 9781398442061 (ePub e-book)

www.austinmacauley.com

First Published 2022
Austin Macauley Publishers Ltd®
1 Canada Square
Canary Wharf
London
E14 5AA

Acknowledgements

Thanks to Diane Bryson for all her advice and guidance
in writing this book.

Foreword

Purposefully he drew her towards him, kissing her passionately while sliding his hand down the length of her spine stopping just above her buttocks. He didn't want her to feel his excitement, not yet, not just yet, not before he knew that she was ready. He didn't have long to wait.

Now their tongues were exploring each other's mouths, hungrily sucking and probing she ran the tip of her tongue across his gums. Suddenly she stabbed at the back of his throat with a sharp prodding movement which imitated the movement of her hips that were now sensually gyrating against his throbbing groin.

The doctor had never known such excitement in foreplay before, and he wanted it to last for as long as possible. Pulling his shirt open, exposing his nipples, she began to explore their circumference with the tips of her long soft fingers, causing a surge of pleasure to engulf his moist body. Now she was the one in command, a totally uninhibited woman who knew the pleasure that he craved and who also knew how to withhold that ultimate pleasure until he begged for its release. Sucking at his earlobe, she tugged and kissed it in a way that he had never known before; causing him to fear that he would lose control, yet there was more to come, much more. Feeling her hand slowly travelling down from his nipples, forever down towards his stomach, stroking and brushing its quivering surface, he gasped at the room's still air as he felt her hand travelling down, forever down.

He knew that she expected him to do something in return, anything that might give her some of the pleasure that she was giving him. Awkwardly, he cupped her breasts within his large soft hands, playing with her nipples until they stood to attention. Circling their circumference in a slow soft movement until he felt her body quiver, he pinched their tips, squeezing their hard little points until she groaned with desire. Now he knew that pain gave her pleasure and her desire encouraged him to increase his roughness; tearing at her clothing, he bit her breasts and scratched at her moist flesh.

The two lovers were now totally consumed within their burning passion, each focussing on the other's desires, consumed with lust, a burning frenzied lust that neither wanted to break by falling onto the double bed.

Faster and faster they urgently tore, bit and pulled at each other's clothes in a frenzied desire until, as one, they fell.

The two lovers, as one, were enjoying illicit sex which made the fruits of their desire taste all the sweeter.

Neither one of them knew or cared that the curtains to their room were open. Neither one of them knew or cared in their illicit frenzy, that across the quiet narrow street that late afternoon, someone was calmly watching their act of adultery, with a cold detached interest.

Chapter One

In the summer of 1942, London was a dark and dangerous place to live. Every night there were the nightly air raids that killed thousands of its residents, yet there was also a danger much darker than most wished to realise. The danger from within came from the predators, the sharks of a torn London. The profiteers and the dregs of society who kept one step ahead of the establishment, and thus became invisible. People often disappeared over night and were presumed killed by enemy action, or perhaps had just moved on in the mayhem of war. No one really questioned the fact that a neighbour hadn't been seen for some time. Very few were missed, and even fewer were reported as missing to the authorities. Even if they were reported, the police were far too busy to investigate. Thanks to the war, a lot of black market profiteers and blackmailers became very rich, and in the days before forensic science, a lot of murderers also escaped punishment. Death and the common sight of corpses lying unclaimed in the street bred a complacency which overpowered basic humanity in the general populace. Even so, there was one such death that caused Inspector Ben Bishop to inhale as was his habit when thinking.

"Can we bag her up now sir?" The young sergeant asked in a flippant tone.

"No, not yet sergeant, do we know her name?"

"No sir, so far we haven't found anything with her name on it, no handbag, nothing."

Inspector Ben Bishop glanced sideways at his young uninterested sergeant before pointing down towards the prostrate body of a young woman in her early twenties. "Do you notice anything familiar about her, sergeant?"

"No, not really sir...should I?"

"Use your eyes, man." He bent his tall frame down towards the still half-naked form that was lying on the cold concrete floor of the half-bombed-out warehouse, pointing at her bruised and blooded head. "Her throat's been cut, just like the last one, and look at her feet. For her feet to be cut about like that, she was running without any shoes. The question that we should be asking ourselves is why? Why did she take them off? Did she take them off while running away from her assailant, or did the murderer take them as a souvenir?"

The sergeant thoughtfully pointed at the dead body with his half-chewed pencil. "The other murder victim didn't have any shoes either, did she, sir?"

"Good, now you're beginning to think, what else can you see?"

"Well, it isn't a robbery gone wrong as she's still wearing her jewellery, and as for her shoes, she may not have lost them while running away from an assailant, she could have lost them while running for cover? It was a bad raid last night, sir."

"What! And then slit her own throat for good measure. I don't think so, sergeant. What's more, she was killed elsewhere."

"How do you know that, sir?"

"Where's the blood, sergeant? For a wound like that, there would be blood everywhere if she had been killed here. No, she was brought here to make it look like she had been killed during the air raid. After all, who would have notice her? No one in that mayhem, and even if she was seen, people would probably assume that she had been injured. No, we have a double murderer on our patch, a psychopath. Christ that's all we bloody need.

"How was she transported here is what you should be asking yourself, detective." A rotund middle-aged pathologist burst into the warehouse, and spoke in a loud tone that vibrated around the concrete walls while carrying a black and battered doctor's bag, that swung from his plump grasp. "Considering a car would be noticed due to the scarcity of such transportation these days, I would say that she was carried here by some other means, wouldn't you?"

"Evening, Arthur." Inspector Bishop stepped aside to allow the pathologist access to the prone figure. "Do you think a woman could do this?"

"Doubt it." He paused while looking closely at the battered head. "It would need a considerable amount of force to batter someone like that, mind you, hell hath no fury, etc."

"Oh come on, Arthur, give me something to go on with…please."

"Well he, or she, is left-handed."

"How on earth do you know that?"

"Her throat, she's been cut from right to the left, see." The pathologist pointed his short index finger towards the gaping wound. "Which means a left-handed killer. I can tell you more when I get her on the table and open her up."

"Oh God, please."

"Sorry, Ben, I forgot about your sensitive stomach. I would have thought with all the bodies you've seen in your life, you would have been used to a spot of blood by now."

"When I get used to the atrocities that mankind can inflict on each other, George, I'll hand my badge in."

Inspector Bishop drew another long deep breath, while stroking his chin in thought. "I want this whole place searched, sergeant." He suddenly snapped before turning to leave. "Everything, do you understand me?

"Yes, sir."

"And Arthur, I want your report on my desk ASAP. If I have a psychopath on my patch, I want to know about it."

"I'll do my best, Ben, you know that, but I can't promise."

"I don't want your promise, Arthur. I want your report, and sergeant, search in particular for her handbag."

"Surely if she was killed elsewhere, sir, the murderer would just dump it."

"Perhaps, yet you never know, sergeant, we might just get lucky. And if you find her shoes, I want to know about them as well." Inspector Bishop called over his shoulder as a sudden cold breeze momentarily caused his raincoat to swirl around his long legs as he briskly walked towards his waiting car.

"Yes, sir."

"What's bitten him, sergeant?"

"Toothache, and his dentist was bombed out last night."

Suddenly, the exhausted men burst into laughter that broke the severity of the scene on which they were all involved; they had to, for that's how they coped with everyday tragedy.

"Well, you'd better do what the man said, sergeant, and start searching the place." Arthur Fellows began to withdraw a handful of plastic exhibit bags from the confines of his leather doctor's bag. "And I'd better start mopping her up." He suddenly fell silent while looking down at the young woman's battered features. "You know, she's a very attractive woman, or was, poor thing."

Sergeant Tipping silently nodded his head in agreement, while seeing yet another late night stretching out before him. Quickly turning towards the uniformed police officer, who was staring down on the unfortunate corpse in a transfixed state, he suddenly felt the desire to seek out the company of a stiff, unauthorised whisky.

"Well you heard the man," Sergeant Tipping snapped, causing the half-asleep officer to physically jump. "I want this whole place searched from top to bottom, and look particularly for her handbag and shoes. They have to be somewhere."

"Yes, sir."

"And don't forget, if you find her bag, I want the contents listed, and on my desk by the end of play today."

"Yes, sir."

"You'll get shot if he finds out, sergeant." Arthur Fellows called after him, while filling the contents of a bag with the deceased's jewellery.

"Well, we'll just have to make sure that he doesn't find out then, won't we, Arthur?"

Sergeant Tipping wearily smiled at the amused pathologist before turning to leave in search of the nearest watering hole that hadn't yet been bombed out of existence. He had a long search.

* * * *

Inspector Bishop crossed his long hands over his flat stomach before leaning back in his old battered swivel chair, silently watching his sergeant type out a long report on the old battered typewriter that clattered noisily on the adjoining desk, before slowly smiling.

"So where did you find her handbag?"

The simple question caused Sergeant Timothy Tipping to look up with a surprised expression which creased his otherwise smooth brow. "It's all in my report, sir; I've placed it on your desk." He now ran his short fingers through his short black hair before rising. "It was found under some rubbish in the alleyway, close to where she was found, sir." Placing the opened file before his boss, he now began to fiddle with the small brown radio that was placed on his boss' desk, until he found the cricket reports of the day's play. "I just can't fathom as to why he didn't just throw it away though, sir. It doesn't make any sense."

"Nothing makes any sense in this case, sergeant. So she didn't just drop it then, it was purposefully hidden, and the question that we need to be asking ourselves, is why? Why was it hidden?"

"Because the killer tried to hide the fact, that he wanted us to find it, sir?" Sergeant Tipping asked.

"Correct, now you're beginning to think like me. Why did he want us to find it is my next question? Will you stop fiddling with that bloody radio sergeant?"

"Sorry, sir."

"Where is it, anyway?"

"Where is what, sir?"

"Her handbag, where is it?"

'With all of her other personal possessions, I'll bring them to you if you want, sir."

"Yes, that would be a good idea." Inspector Bishop looked up at his sergeant who was standing in deep thought while listening to the cricket report. "Anytime now will do, sergeant, if you can spare the time that is?"

"Oh, sorry, sir."

"Before you go, what about her shoes? Were they ever found?"

"No, sir, they weren't found, we looked everywhere."

"You looked everywhere, did you, sergeant? Well, I guess the chances of your finding them where you were looking were pretty slim."

Sergeant Tipping's expression mirrored the shock that had suddenly overwhelmed him. "Sir?" He finally replied in a questioning tone, his mouth feeling surprisingly dry.

"Look, sergeant, it's my job to know what goes on, and if my sergeant delegates my orders to a police constable as soon as my back's turned, and then slides off to the local pub, I will know about it before he even has time to sit down, do you understand me?"

"Yes, sir. Who told you, sir?"

"It doesn't matter who told me, sergeant, the only thing that matters to you is the fact that I know." His firm voice sounded tired yet his gaze held that of the chastised man, who stood subdued, in front of him. "You can consider yourself lucky this time, yet if you do it again, I'll take the skin off your arse. Get my drift?"

"Yes, sir. Sorry sir."

"Now, go and fetch me that bag and anything else that belonged to her, perhaps then we may find the answer as to why he hid it and not just got rid of it, and even more important, whether we can find any connection with the other murder. It has the same pattern, throat slit and no shoes."

Sergeant Tipping, feeling berated yet relieved that his boss was in a charitable mood, turned quickly to leave his accuser.

"Oh and while you're out of the office," Inspector Bishop called after him. "Get me a coffee with plenty of sugar, and don't use that Goddamned awful powdered milk." He gently touched his swollen cheek. "This bloody toothache is killing me."

* * * *

An hour later, Inspector Bishop tentatively sipped at the hot coffee while swallowing several painkillers. He sighed while gently rubbing his swollen cheek before glancing up at his sergeant who was reading the pathology report.

"She had eaten a full meal of lamb and some sort of potato several hours before she died." His voice was low and held a questioning tone. "She also had intercourse and it wasn't rape, sir, it was, you know, consensual."

"The functions of the human body are an enigma to you, aren't they, sergeant? I would never believe that you were a married man."

Sergeant Tipping smiled sheepishly before handing the report over to his boss, who had by now swallowed two more painkillers.

"Which in my book means what, sergeant?" Ben Bishop looked up at his sergeant and smiled while reaching up for the proffered report.

"She was either out on the town, or working the streets, sir."

"Exactly, now all we need to do is to find out who she was, and who she was with."

"Perhaps she was single, sir."

"Doubt it. Even with her throat cut, she was still pretty. No, she was married alright, I'd put my pension on it. Did the report say whether she had any children?"

"No, sir, no. Never had any children."

"No," Inspector Bishop replied in a thoughtful tone, before suddenly throwing the report down onto his cluttered desk. "Okay, where's the contents of her handbag?"

"I think it's under here, sir." Sergeant Tipping quickly rummaged through several piles of loose papers on his boss' desk before triumphantly holding up the contents of the deceased's handbag that were confined within a small see-through plastic bag. Inspector Bishop quickly tore open the bag which enabled its contents to spill noisily onto his desk.

"One lipstick." His quiet voice held a thoughtful tone as he placed each item separately in front of him. "One set of keys."

"I would like to know what door they opened, sir."

"So would I, sergeant." Ben Bishop looked up at his sergeant and briefly smiled before placing the keys to one side. "One purse." Suddenly he tipped the purse's contents out, causing the coins to clatter noisily onto his desk. "What's this?" Unzipping a small apartment that was concealed within the purse's interior, he pulled out a tiny piece of paper that was folded into a square. Quickly unfolding the tantalising find, he read outload its secret. "8.30. 23 Browning Street. Doctor Dwyer."

Both men looked incredulously at each other before Ben Bishop suddenly rose, tipping his chair to one side in the process.

"Come on, sergeant, I think it's time that we pay Doctor Dwyer a visit."

Chapter Two

Doctor Brian Dwyer looked over his desk towards his receptionist and smiled as his eyes rested upon her full breasts. One day, he thought, that button will give up the will to live and fly from its anchor, revealing what he had been dreaming about for the past six months. The very thought of her breasts tumbling out of her uniform's confinement made his groin ache with desire, which caused him to shift his buttocks within the worn swivel chair.

"Miss Sharp." He spoke quietly, revealing nothing of his inner turmoil. "Who is my next patient?"

"Mr Whitton, Doctor. You are late with your list today, so he has been waiting for some time."

"Did you explain why?"

"Yes, Doctor. He understood when I explained that you had been called away on an emergency."

"Good, thank you, nurse. Show him in, would you, please?"

"Yes, Doctor."

He watched her hips sway as she walked towards his surgery door. *Bloody hell*, he thought quietly to himself. A man could get seasick watching those hips. Smiling, his thoughts drifted momentarily back to the previous evening. How he would love to experience the same sex with her as he had done with Julie. How he would love to slowly travel down the length of her flat stomach with the tip of his moist tongue, forever down until he finally reached his goal. Just for one night, he would like to spread her legs and – the knock on the door brought him out of his thoughts. "Come!" He barked, annoyed at the interruption.

"Doctor Dwyer?" His features mirroring the shock he felt upon seeing two unknown men, flashing their ID badges as they advanced towards him, entering his surgery. "Are you a Doctor Brian Dwyer, sir?"

"Yes, yes, I'm Doctor Dwyer, who are you gentlemen, and why are you here?"

"May I introduce myself? I am Inspector Bishop and this is my sergeant, Sergeant Tipping. We won't take up much of your time, sir." Ben Bishop indicated his head towards the two chairs that were positioned in front of the doctor's desk. "May we sit down, sir?"

"Yes, yes, of course. I hope you won't be too long, officers, I'm behind with my list today. Now what's all this about?"

"You're behind with your list today, sir, now why might that be?"

"Well if it's anything to do with you, officer, I was called away on an emergency."

"Were you, indeed? What sort of an emergency might that be, sir?"

"Now look here, officer, will you please come to the point and explain to me why you're here?"

"Can you please tell us where you were at 8.30 last night, sir?"

Doctor Dwyer's face turned red, a detail that didn't go un-noticed by Ben Bishop. "I was here of course, catching up on some paperwork. You can ask my nurse, if you wish."

"We already have, sir. She told us that the air raid started at around 7 pm, and you told her to go home early. Have you forgotten that, sir?"

"Oh yes, I remember that now, yes of course I did. I'm sorry, I still don't understand what business it is of yours though, officer."

"You may not be aware of the fact that a young lady was murdered last night, sir. She was found a couple of blocks away from your surgery in the early hours of this morning."

"Good God! Well I'm sorry to hear that, that's tragic. I'm sorry, yet I still don't understand what that has got to do with me."

Inspector Bishop paused for maximum effect while studying the doctor's expression intensely. "She had your name and this address in her purse. She was meeting you **here** at 8.30 yesterday evening, now why would that be if you were here, as you say, alone, doing paperwork?"

The doctor quickly looked between Ben Bishop and his sergeant who was busy writing in his small black notebook, before lowering his head in defeat. "The stupid, stupid bitch."

"I want her name, sir."

"No, no names…please."

"I must insist, sir, I want her name now! By the way, do you collect shoes?"

The sudden and unexpected question caused Brian Dwyer to look up sharply in disbelief. "No, no of course not, what sort of question is that? Look, you don't understand, officer. I'm a married man. Oh God, this doesn't have to become public knowledge, does it?" He now held Ben Bishop's steady gaze with a pleading expression. "My family, my practice, this could ruin me."

"I want her name, sir, and I want it now. I must insist."

"No, no, please. I can't give names."

"Then I'm afraid, we will have to take you down to the station where we can interview you on a more formal basis."

"No, no, please, that won't be necessary. Her name is, her name was, Julie, Julie Jackson."

"Do you know where she lived?"

"Yes, I believe it was 4A Cuff House, Greyhound Lane."

"What do you mean you believe? Was it or wasn't it?"

Brian Dwyer shrugged his shoulders in a matter of fact way. "Yes, that was her address. I went to see her there a couple of times, that's all. It was a bit of a dump really, so I preferred her to come here."

"Did you bother to ask whether she was married or not, sir?" Timothy Tipping looked up from his notepad, his facial expression mirroring his disgust.

"I think she was once, she did say that her husband had been killed in action somewhere. I'm sorry, I wasn't really listening."

"I bet you weren't. Did she mention whether or not she had any children?"

"I believe not, yet as I said, I wasn't paying much attention to what she was saying at the time. I wish I had now. I'm sorry. You must think that I'm a right bastard."

"It's not up to me to express an opinion, sir. How often did you see her?"

"Every week, perhaps more if I…"

"If you what, sir?"

"If I wanted her…Oh God, I can't believe this is happening. How was she, I mean, how was she killed?"

"She was—"

"I'm afraid we can't divulge that information, sir." Ben Bishop quickly interrupted his sergeant. "It's confidential, you understand."

"Yes, I understand...of course."

"How did you get to know her?"

"Like you get to know any tart, in bars, on the streets, it's easy if you know where to look."

"Where did you pick her up?"

"As I said, in a bar, it's called The Black Swan. It's only a couple of blocks away. You probably know it."

"Can't say that I do, sir, was she the only one?"

"What do you mean, was she the only one?"

"Well, sir, she was obviously a prostitute. Was she the only woman that you have paid to have sex with?"

"No...no she wasn't."

"I want their names, sir."

"I honestly can't give you any more names. Julie was my only regular girl that I saw every week, the others I just picked up as and when I wanted to be entertained. They were only one-offs, for want of a better phrase. We never entered into niceties."

"I don't think that I need to remind you about the dangers of casual sex, sir."

"Why should that worry me, Inspector? I could be killed anytime in an air raid. You live life for today. Tomorrow may never come."

Ben Bishop slowly rose from the hard chair, while signalling for his sergeant to follow. "I'm sorry, sir; you will have to come down to the station with us for further questioning under caution."

"No, no, I can't do that. God, I have a surgery full of patients. I can't just leave them and go off with you. I can't just leave, it's ridiculous."

"Tell me, sir." Ben Bishop motioned his head towards a wooden crucifix that hung on the wall behind him. "You keep mentioning God, are you a religious man?"

"I was, I'm a cradle Catholic, Inspector. I mean I was born into the religion."

"Obviously you are a lapsed Catholic now, sir, a married man having extra-marital affairs. What would your God say?"

"Don't you dare mock me, you have no idea what I have to put up with in my marriage."

"It's still a sin, sir, even for a fallen Catholic."

"Yes, it is, yet only God has the right to judge me, Inspector, not even my brother has that right, and certainly not you."

"Your brother? Why should you worry about your brother?"

"He's the priest at St Joseph's; the pride of the family is my brother. He can't do anything wrong." Looking up, he smiled briefly at Inspector Bishop, before rising. "That's where I was this morning, that's the real reason why I was late. I was in the confessional, confessing to my sins. My brother likes me to confess my sins, even though I'm beyond redemption."

* * * *

"You can wait outside and guard the door if you don't mind, sir." Inspector Bishop smiled down at the scruffy landlord who drew heavily upon a long expired cigarette.

"I think I'd like to come in with you if you don't mind."

"I'm sorry, sir, I do mind. Now if you would be good enough just to stand here, we won't be long." Sergeant Tipping quickly opened the flimsy wooden door, just as Inspector Bishop turned to walk into the dimly lit room.

"Well, we have found the door that the keys belonged to, sir."

"Yes, sergeant, we have."

"Can you remind me again, what we're supposed to be looking for, sir?"

"Anything that ties Dwyer into the murders, a diary would be nice. Then we would know when and where they met for sex. It might also give us some other leads. You start over there, and I'll look in the wardrobe."

The two men seemed to make the small room feel even smaller as Sergeant Tipping searched through the bedside cabinet that stood beside the single bed that had been covered with a dusty quilt. The old wooden wardrobe that dominated one side of the room attracted

Inspector Bishop's attention. Scanning the dimly lit room, he made his way towards it, before opening the doors wide.

"Pull the curtains open, will you, sergeant? Let's get some light in here."

"Yes, sir."

There wasn't a bathroom as that was situated on the floor below, for the use of all the buildings occupants. Sergeant Tipping drew the curtains, which were coated in thick brick dust from the previous night's bombings, only to find a pane of broken glass. Everything was covered with brick dust, even the small sink with its single bar of soap and toothbrush felt grimy to the touch.

"I can't find anything of interest, sir. This must be a photograph of her husband though." Sergeant Tipping held up a framed photograph of a young soldier in uniform.

"You surmise it is, sergeant. Even if it is, it doesn't help us. Keep looking." Ben Bishop glanced at his sergeant while searching through the pockets of a worn coat. "There has to be something to say that she existed here. Poor girl, when she hung this coat up, she doubtless thought that one day she would be wearing it again."

"What about these, sir?" Sergeant Tipping held up a pair of silk stockings which caused Inspector Bishop to whistle.

"Nice, except all that it tells us is that she had a generous benefactor."

"Probably an American GI. They have all the luck."

"All the luck and all the money, such is life. Look through that chest of drawers, there may be something in there."

Moments passed without either man speaking, the only sound came from the movement of drawers opening and closing and the grunts of the inpatient landlord who was still waiting outside in the corridor.

"Sir?" Sergeant Tipping voice held a questioning tone as he slowly withdrew from her underwear drawer, a small black leather-bound address book. "Is this what we were looking for?"

"It certainly could be. Well done, sergeant. Come on, let's get the hell out of here."

Chapter Three

Ellen Cooper, an attractive slightly-built middle aged woman, elegantly alighted from the hissing steam train, as it slowly pulled into King's Cross railway station. She had been a war widow for over two years now and as such had become used to wearing black, and why not. It was her favourite colour and she enjoyed the respectability that widowhood afforded her. Her husband, Colin Cooper, had died early in the war, so early in fact that he hadn't even had the time to fire a shot at the Hun. Nevertheless, that was her secret. To the world, she was a respectable war widow, and for that status alone, she secretly thanked Colin, for the marriage had otherwise been childless and loveless. She looked around while trying to locate an exit that would bring her out to the taxi rank.

"Can I help you, madam?"

A man's deep voice caused her to jump before turning towards the young porter, who was smiling down at her while touching the peak of his porter's cap.

"Oh thank you, yes, yes, I'm trying to find the exit for the taxi rank. It's so difficult with all these people scurrying around. I get so flustered."

"Don't fret yourself about that, madam; you just leave everything to me. I will get you there in a jiffy, that I will. Now, if you will permit me." He indicated towards her heavy suitcase. "I will carry your case for you."

"Oh yes, thank you, you're most kind."

It wasn't long before she found herself seated in the back of a black taxicab, heading through the crowded streets of London. She was shocked when she passed the bomb sites and witnessed people searching through the rubble for their lost belongings. It was all too much for her refined senses, and she chose not to look. Closing her eyes, and taking a deep breath, she forced herself to think of nice things, like strawberries and ice cream on a long hot summer's afternoon, until she had finally reached her destination, the vicarage of St Joseph's.

"Ellen, my dear, how wonderful to see you." She opened her eyes to see her old school friend hurrying towards her, with her arms outstretched in welcome. Mary, a tall slender woman, who had just seen her brother, Father John Dwyer, off for the mid-day service, smiled broadly. "I didn't think that you would ever get here, we had an awful air raid last night, and you've even managed to get a taxi. Why, you're just marvellous, my dear."

"No, I'm afraid to disappoint you, this has nothing to do with me. It was the porter at the station who flagged him down. I had to tip him rather well though, yet it was worth every penny, I reckon I would still be standing there if it wasn't for him. This burly chap tried to force his way past me, the scoundrel. Yet the porter stood his ground and pushed me in first. He slammed the door shut so fast he almost caught the chap's foot in the process. He was marvellous, such bravery in the face of adversity. I haven't had as much fun since I was a girl. I tell you, Mary, we could do with more like him. We would soon beat the Hun."

"Oh how marvellous, what fun you've had. Come in, come in, and we can have a good natter over luncheon."

It wasn't long before the two women were seated within their respective armchairs, drinking tea and eating triangular sandwiches without the crusts, of course. Ellen subconsciously frowned as she wondered why her friend had summoned her. She hadn't heard from Mary in weeks, yet three days ago, the telephone rang and Mary had asked her to come down and stay with her for a couple of weeks. Well, that was it. That was what she said, a couple of weeks, just like that. So putting her annoyance to one side, as she didn't relish travelling into a warzone, not even for her friend, she packed her case and caught the next train into London as she couldn't resist the intrigue. She now put her hands neatly onto her lap, looked Mary straight in the eyes, and blurted out what had been puzzling her.

"Mary, my dear, don't you think it's time that you explained to me why you have invited me down to stay with you?"

"Oh Ellen, there has been such trouble, I need your advice."

"Well, couldn't you have asked for my advice over the telephone, dear? It's lovely to see you and all that, yet bringing me all the way down here to London of all places, just to ask for my advice is a bit much, don't you think?"

"Please don't be annoyed with me, Ellen, I know I have asked a lot of you, asking you to come here with such dangers and everything, yet Ellen, you're so wise, and I am so worried."

"Tell me, my dear, what on earth is troubling you?" Ellen reached out to touch her friend's hand, which instantly held hers in a tight grasp.

"It's Valerie, you remember her? She's Brian's wife."

"Yes, I remember her, what about her?"

There was a long pause before Mary spoke. "She's been receiving these poison pen letters. Terrible things have been said to her. She's been accused of all sorts of things that are not true. She always has been a bag of nerves, yet all this has made her positively suicidal."

"Oh dear…What sort of things?"

"She won't say."

"Has she gone to the police?"

"Well, that's just it, she won't hear of it. She says that she will only make matter worse for Brian."

"Brian? Why? Why would it involve him?"

"Apparently these letters implicate him in some way." She shook her head slightly. "I don't know."

"No. neither do I. Mary. But I do know one thing; I know that you're not telling me everything. Now if you want me to help you, I suggest you tell me now, how is he involved?"

"Oh Ellen, I don't know where to begin." She quickly fumbled for her small handkerchief which was tucked up her long sleeve. "There have been terrible things going on here, terrible things, and the police suspect Brian. They haven't charged him as yet, but they will do, I'm sure of it."

"Now, Mary, you must be straight with me. What things?"

"Oh, I can't barely say it, awful things."

"For God's sake, Mary, stop being such a baby and tell me before I lose my patience." Ellen felt a surge of annoyance that was becoming increasingly difficult to suppress.

"Alright, I'll tell you. Two prostitutes that Brian has had an association with have been murdered, and the police think that he did it. They marched him out of his surgery in front of all his patients last week; the whole neighbourhood is talking about it."

"I bet they are."

"They questioned him for two days, before they let him go. But I know they'll take him in again, I just know it."

"What do you mean when you said that he's had an association with these women? Was he paying for their services?"

"Yes, yes, unfortunately he was. God, the shame of it all, Ellen." Suddenly she rose and walking over to the fireplace, lit a black market cigarette while looking at her own image in the large gold framed mirror. "He was always the odd one out in the family." She continued while sending clouds of white smoke billowing into the still air. "Even if he is a doctor, yet this, this surpasses everything."

Ellen looked down at her hands and sighed. "Didn't his first wife die under suspicious circumstances?"

"That's just what I mean." She quickly returned to her seat, stubbing out the long cigarette in the glass ashtray that was permanently placed by the side of her chair. "He said that she used to go swimming in that canal. But I didn't believe him then, and I don't believe him now."

"He was never charged, Mary, the coroner recorded death by misadventure. What makes you think he was wrong?"

"Oh come on, Ellen, who would go swimming in a filthy canal? If you believe that, you'll believe anything."

"Well, people do odd things, Mary; you shouldn't doubt your own brother."

"Well, I do, Ellen. My main concern is John. He's worried stiff by all this and he's just so busy with his parish work, it's not fair on him; or Valerie, come to that. I don't know, every woman he's come into contact with, all through his life, have died."

"Yes…most odd." Ellen spoke with a slow soft tone. "I wonder why."

"I dread to think."

"Well, my dear, I'll stay to keep you company if you so wish, yet I am unable to interfere, apart from saying that Valerie, or at the very least, you, should go to the police at once, and tell them about these letters without any further delay."

"Tell the police what?" Father John Dwyer, a short rotund priest entered the room with a smile that was directed towards Ellen, who in turn declined her head in acknowledgment.

"Oh, hello, dear." Mary began to pour a third cup of tea out of the large china tea pot. "I've saved you some tea. How is your sermon coming along?"

"Slowly, I'm afraid."

"Well, don't make it too long, dear. Last week I had to wake Mrs Wobble Hat up, she was almost sliding off her chair, poor woman."

Father Dwyer smiled, before fidgeting with his dog collar that always chaffed his bulbous neck. "Heaven forbid such a sight."

They all laughed quietly, yet the uneasy feeling, which engulfed Ellen while slowly sipping her tea, never left her.

Chapter Four

Valerie Dwyer, a middle-aged woman who looked all of her sixty years, sighed while looking at her own reflection in the hallway mirror. "I really must do something about my hair." She subconsciously touched her short curls that were once her best feature, before stooping to pick the morning post up from the floor. "Oh good, there may finally be some news about my Ruthie." She spoke quietly to her invisible companion who constantly kept her company, while placing the post onto the hallway table. "I'm going to have a cup of coffee to celebrate. Would you like a cup of coffee?"

She received an unheard reply, unheard that is, to anyone else apart from herself while she duly made two cups of coffee. Placing them onto the breakfast table, she slowly retrieved the unopened post. "I had better open these now, don't you think? There may be some news about my Ruthie…Ruth." She repeated in a soft whisper before wiping away a stubborn tear that rolled down her white cheek. "My darling Ruthie is coming home, you know. One day she'll come home, I know she will, she wouldn't leave me, she loves me too much, she wouldn't hurt me. Not my Ruthie."

With a plate of biscuits which she pushed towards her companion, she took a deep breath while beginning to open the few letters that were now scattered before her. The disappointment which she felt with every letter that held no news of Ruth's homecoming twisted her heart until she couldn't breathe. "Perhaps, the next letter will hold news of Ruthie". Frantically tearing open the last letter, she could feel the blood draining away from her as her gaze scanned the large black handwriting that was scrawled across the large white paper. "No…no, it's not true," She whispered while her hands, which felt numb with shock, uncontrollably shook, causing the neatly folded letter to fall from her grasp. *"It's not true"*. She finally shouted to her invisible companion. ***"Ruthie."***

* * * *

It had been a long tiring day for Doctor Brian Dwyer yet he was thankful that some of his older patients still wanted to see him, as he had lost half of his practice and still counting. The reasons were numerous, yet it all boiled down to the fact that he was the prime suspect in two murders and his patients no longer trusted him. Putting his head in his hands, he outwardly groaned while thinking about the long hard years that he had studied for his degree. He had such hopes, such dreams.

43

His thoughts drifted back to his first wife and the time that they had come to London from Braintree to start his practice. People flocked to the young handsome doctor who had just qualified. How happy they both were, yet their happiness didn't last for long. Disaster always strikes, always. Just as he finds happiness, disaster strikes.

"Are you alright, Doctor? Is there anything that I can do for you?" Miss Sharp spoke in a soft enquiring tone which caused the doctor to smile briefly.

"You may have been able to do something for me once, nurse, but not now."

"I'm sorry, Doctor?"

"It doesn't matter, nurse. I'm sorry, I was being flippant. No, thank you, there isn't anything that you can do for me now. You can go home and I'll see you in the morning. If we're not bombed out that is, and we still have some patients left."

"Yes, we do seem to have lost a couple of patients, Doctor, yet I'm sure they will return in due course."

"Yes, I'm sure you're right. Good night, nurse."

"Good night, Doctor."

She quietly closed the door behind her, leaving Brian Dwyer alone with his thoughts. Wondering how he could face yet another evening with Valerie and her invisible companion, who always took her side against him. He ran his long slender hands through his brown hair and sighed. He couldn't tell her that her companion was all in her mind, as countless better doctors than him had tried and failed to do in the past. He couldn't tell her that his love for her had died on the day that Ruth had left them, as his heart too, had been broken on that fateful day, and she had been too wrapped up in her own grief to notice his pain. Yet, above all, he couldn't tell her that he wanted to leave her, he couldn't, as it had all been his fault, as she so often reminded him, and he had to stay and see it through. The telephone suddenly rang, jolting him out of his depressive thoughts.

"Dwyer."

"Brian, is that you?"

"Oh hello, John, what's the matter, you sound as if one of your bell ringers has got stuck in the belfry." He laughed, which he knew, sounded out of place.

"No, worse than that. It's Valerie. Brian, you need to come home straight away."

Chapter Five

"You'll never guess, sir!" Sergeant Tipping burst into Ben Bishop's office waving a sheet of foolscap. "There's been another one."

"Another what?"

"Murder…well suicide actually, yet it's tied up with our chap, the doctor. It's his wife; she was just being delivered to the mortuary as I came up here. Apparently she received a poison pen letter this morning, and it tipped her over the edge. I was told that she slit her own throat."

"Bloody hell."

"I know, something must have upset her."

"Well, that's bloody obvious, sergeant, even I can work that one out."

Sergeant Tipping smiled briefly, before placing the report onto Ben Bishop's desk for his inspection.

"Shall we pick him up now, sir?"

"Pick who up?"

"The doctor, of course, he has to be involved in it somehow."

"Has he? No, not yet, he can wait until I'm ready for him." Ben Bishop spoke without looking up from the sheet of close-typed report. "Something just doesn't smell right to me."

"What do you mean, sir? Two murdered women had affairs with him, and now his wife's dead. It can't be a coincidence."

"I know, everything points to him, and that's what's troubling me. What about the shoes? Now we searched his house, and his surgery, from top to bottom and found nothing. Then there was that handbag. It was pretty convenient, wasn't it, that she wrote his name and address down for us to find. No, we were meant to find that bag."

"Well, she could have written his name down as a reminder."

"No, you're not thinking. He told us that he's been seeing her every week for the past six months. Now why should she write his name down? She had no need too. She bloody knew him."

"Then what about the first murder victim, sir?

"Same modus operandi, she knew him, yet only for sex and nothing else. No, he had no need to kill them."

"Not unless…"

"Unless what, sergeant?"

"Unless they wanted a little bit more of the action, perhaps they wanted him to get rid of his wife so that they could move in and play happy families. They put the pressure on, and the dear doctor snapped. I've seen it before, sir."

"Yes…and so have I, yet I have a feeling that we are thinking the way the murderer wants us to think, and I don't like obliging." Suddenly, he rose from his chair. "I want all the prostitutes interviewed. I want to know if any of them had sex with him. Come on, sergeant, I can't just sit here. Let's see what Arthur has to tell us about the new addition. At the very least, I can nick some of his painkillers."

"Tooth still troubling you, sir?"

"Yes, bloody thing, at least I've finally found a dentist that's willing to pull the damn thing out."

* * * *

"Morning Arthur." Inspector Bishop burst into the mortuary while being closely followed by Sergeant Tipping.

"Christ, Ben! You're quick off the mark. I haven't even unwrapped her yet."

"Well, you know me, Arthur. Always eager."

"You won't be so eager when I start cutting her up, will you?" Arthur Fellows smiled while menacingly holding a scalpel up for all to see.

"There's no need for that, is there, Arthur? Word is she committed suicide."

"That's for me to determine, and for you to find out. In the meantime, you can come back in a couple of hours. Unless you want to assist me, of course."

"No, thanks, Arthur. I'll leave all that in your capable hands. We'll come back later."

"By the way, Ben. Before you go, I have some up-to-date news to tell you concerning the first victim."

"Oh, what's that?" Ben Bishop turned suddenly upon his heels.

"She hadn't eaten before she died…apart, that is, for a small quantity of wine and some sort of bread. It could be a wafer."

"What are you trying to tell me, Arthur?"

"I'm trying to tell you, that I believe she had Holy Communion before she died. There's no other explanation. As to where, and when, well, the 'where' is up to you to find out my friend, and as to 'when', I'd say roughly two hours before she died."

"Thanks, Arthur, you're a pal. Come on, sergeant, you're right, let's pick him up."

* * * *

Mary and John Dwyer never argued. They led a quiet orderly life as brother and sister, which Mary Dwyer jealously protected. She didn't want her perfectly respectable world interrupted or threatened in any way, yet today was different. Today Mary Dwyer was incensed that her wayward brother Brian, the talk of the village, had come to stay at the vicarage, and worse, the brother that she had always shielded from any negative forces which threatened to tarnish his good reputation, was in total agreement. Today was the day that she needed to stand firm, she needed to stand firm, against the brother that she so dearly loved.

"I don't want him living here with us, John. I'm not having it."

"Please, Mary, he can hear you."

"I don't care if he can hear me, he's trouble and I don't want him in this house. Unlike him, you have a standing in this community, a standing that people look up to. What will they think when they find out that he's living here?"

"People will think that we are doing our Christian duty by taking in one of our family who is grieving."

"Grieving? He's not grieving, John. Those tears are for his own shame…his own guilt."

"Mary, please."

"Don't you *Mary please me*; he's paid for prostitutes, John, while his wife was ill in bed. No wonder the poor woman killed herself."

"Mary please, that's enough."

"No, it's not enough. Nowhere near enough, I am not having a man like that under this roof, and that's final."

"I'm sorry." Ellen Cooper tentatively entered the sparse kitchen. "I'm sorry to interrupt you, but can you please keep your voices down? Brian is so distraught; he says that he's going to go back to his own house."

"Good, sooner the better, that's what I say. Does he need any help in packing?"

"Oh, Mary, how can you be so hard on your own brother?"

"Easy, when he has the morals of a tomcat."

They were suddenly brought out of their heated debate by several thunderously loud, consecutive knocks on the front door.

"That sounds like the police."

"Well, it certainly doesn't sound like the milk man. I'll get it." Father John Dwyer subconsciously touched his dog collar while walking slowly towards the old-fashioned wooden door.

"Yes, can I help you?"

"I am Inspector Bishop, and this is my sergeant, Sergeant Timothy Tipping." Holding up their ID cards, Ben Bishop held the priest in a steady gaze. "May we come in, please, sir?" Ben Bishop didn't wait for the priest to reply, he only pushed passed him. Glancing at the two startled women, who stood at the entrance of the kitchen in shock, he now made his way straight into the sitting room where Brian Dwyer stood, Ben Bishop once more flashed his warrant card.

"Mr Brian Dwyer."

"Yes, you know I am."

"I would like you to accompany us to the station, please, sir."

"Why, I've told you everything I know, this is ridiculous."

"Now please, sir, I must insist."

"Don't worry, Brian." John Dwyer flustered. "I'll get our solicitor to come down."

"That would be a very good idea, sir, and while you're at it, you can tell him to bring some partners. Your brother is going to need all the help that he can get."

Chapter Six

Ellen Cooper walked up the long pathway to the church's main entrance. It had been a warm day so she hadn't bothered to put her coat on. She was beginning to regret that decision now though, as a cool breeze began to swirl around her. Pushing against the tall oak doors, she slowly entered the church's gloomy interior, noticing as she did, a large crucifix with the bloodied Christ looking down on her. She didn't like these types of churches as they always made her feel cold and afraid.

"Ello, can I 'elp ya?"

"Oh, hello, yes, yes, I hope you can." She felt flustered, unprepared, as she looked into the kindly eyes of a middle-aged rotund woman, who was wearing a small straw hat with small yellow daisies around its rim. "I'm trying to find the Curate. Is he around anywhere?"

"No, I'm sorry, me dear, he ain't. Can I be of any 'elp?"

"Perhaps you can, I don't really know." Ellen smiled briefly before stepping closer to the unknown woman. "May I ask to whom am I speaking?"

"Oh, don't you worry about me now, dear." She threw her hands up in mock surprise. "Me name's Mrs Jenkins, I've worked 'ere for years so I 'ave. There ain't much that I don't know about, I can tell ya that. Now how can I 'elp ya dear?"

"Well, you know that I'm staying with Father Dwyer and his sister at the Vicarage?"

"Yes, dear, that's right. I've seen ya around."

"Well, I don't know very much about the brother, Brian Dwyer, is that his name?"

"That's right, dear, that's 'is name."

"Would it be possible for you to tell me something about him?"

"Well now, I know plenty, dear." She shook her head which caused the little hat to perilously vibrate on the top of her greying head. "Yet yu want gossip, and that's one thing that I ain't prepared to give yu. Not against Father Dwyer I ain't, anyway. No, no, if yu want gossip, you'll have to go elsewhere for it."

"No, please, you misunderstand me, Mrs Jenkins. I'm sorry if I have given you the wrong impression. I only want to know about the brother, Brian Dwyer. I am not asking about Father Dwyer. I promise, I will not ask you any questions about him."

"As I told yu before, dear, I ain't gossiping. Now if yu want to know anything about the church or the times of the services, I'm your man. Apart from that, I'm not."

Once more, she shook her head which caused Ellen to fear for her hat's survival.

"Okay, then can you at least tell me who I can speak to?"

"Ya, I can do that alright."

"Well, who can I speak too then?"

"Yu can speak to the old priest, Father Michael; he used to be the priest 'ere when they were serving boys. He knew them well, did Father Michael."

"Where can I find him?"

"'E's in the retirement 'ome for priests. If yu come with me into the vestry, I'll give yu the address. You'll have to make an appointment first though. They don't just see anyone."

"No, I understand that, thank you for your time. By the way, do you know that your hat is about to fall off"?

Mrs Jenkins smiled while pushing her hat further onto the top of her head. "Oh aye, dear, it always is, yet like me, it'll survive."

* * * *

Inspector Bishop and Sergeant Tipping sat on the opposite side of the table, facing Brian Dwyer who looked tired and beaten by the recent events. The interview room was sparse and, apart from the table and four chairs, held no furniture.

"You know why you're here, Dwyer?" Ben Bishop spoke in a solemn tone.

"No, to be honest, I don't. I've told you guys everything that I know. What more do you want?"

"The truth would be a good place to start."

"I've told you the truth."

"Have you? You didn't tell us about your first wife drowning, did you? You conveniently forgot to tell us about that." Leaning towards his sergeant, who was busy taking notes, he slowly repeated. "He forgot to tell us about that, didn't he, sergeant?"

"He certainly did, sir. He certainly forgot to tell us about his wife drowning."

"I didn't think that it was relevant. It's happened over twenty years ago, for God's sake."

"How did it happen, Dwyer?"

"For some reason, she always liked swimming in the canal. I used to warn her of the dangers, yet she never listened to me." He sighed before drawing deeply on his hand rolled cigarette. "Anyway, one day, I think it was on a Saturday, she was late home. I searched everywhere for her, I was frantic. In the end, I called you guys. You must have the details in your report."

"Oh yes, we've got the details all right, haven't we, sergeant?"

"Certainly have, sir."

"That's how we knew…we looked you up you see, and it was all there Dwyer…you received over £5,000 life insurance after your wife died. You needed that money to finance your practice, didn't you?"

"Yes, I could have done with the money; the practice was doing well and I would have liked to make some improvements, that's all. I wasn't about to kill my wife for it though."

"You killed her, didn't you, Dwyer? You killed her for that money, then you thought that you had got away with it once, so you'll try your luck again."

"No...no I never killed her, we were happy I tell you."

"Were you? Then conveniently along comes wife number two, how much was she insured for, Dwyer, what's your blood money this time?"

"No...no...it's nothing like that."

"Then tell us what it's like. Tell us why your two wives have died under suspicious circumstances. Tell us why they were both insured up to their necks, then you can tell us why a so-called happily married man needs the services of prostitutes who just happen to get themselves murdered."

The room fell eerily silent, as Brian Dwyer stubbed his cigarette butt out onto a round tin ash tray.

"I'm waiting, Dwyer."

"Everything that you have said is true. I did insure my wives, we insured each other, just in case, whoever was left would be okay financially. We were happy for a time, until we lost our daughter, Ruth. She was our only child. She was fourteen at the time." His voice faltered while he tried to control his uncontrollable emotions. "It was on a warm summer's evening and she decided to go to see her friend, she took her bicycle. She was so beautiful, my heart ached with pride when I looked at her."

"Can we just get to the point, Dwyer?"

"The point being, she never reached her friend's house. She was killed by a hit-and-run driver. She died instantly." He looked Ben Dwyer in the eyes before whispering. "Have you got that in your report, inspector?"

"No."

"No…they never caught who did it. The problem is that my wife could never accept that Ruth wasn't coming home anymore. She was always looking for her, always expecting her to walk through the door. She even cooked for an imaginary friend. Have you any idea what it was like to live with someone like that?"

"What was different yesterday, what caused her to take her own life?"

"My brother found her. He told me that she had received a poison pen letter saying that Ruth had never loved us and that she wasn't ever coming home."

"Where's this so-called letter?"

"He destroyed it; he said that he didn't want me to see it, as it was too distressing."

"That's convenient."

"It's true, I tell you."

"The fact still remains; you used prostitutes while your wife was ill. We've spoken to them, Dwyer…they know you, you're a regular on their patch."

"I have needs, needs that my wife couldn't fulfil."

"You disgust me."

"I disgust myself, yet I'm no killer, inspector. Those women left me alive."

"What did you do with their shoes, Dwyer?"

"Why do you keep going on about shoes? I don't know anything about shoes."

"Where have you hidden their shoes, come on, own up to it, Dwyer…you killed those women because they wanted more, much more, and you snapped."

"You have searched my house and my surgery from top to bottom yet found nothing to incriminate me. That's what you can't take, isn't it? You can't prove that it was me who killed those women."

"How did you transport their bodies after you killed them, Dwyer? How did you clean all that blood up, because there was plenty of it."

"How many more times do I have to tell you? I haven't killed anyone."

"I don't believe you."

"Then charge me, and if you don't charge me, I have every right to leave here."

"You're not going anywhere, Dwyer, apart from a prison cell." Ben Bishop's voice held a menacing tone as he leant over the table towards the exhausted doctor. "I know you murdered your wives and those other women; I know you did it, Dwyer, we have Julie Jenkin's diary. We know how many times you met, when you met, and how much you paid her. I know you did it, Dwyer, and you can be damn sure I won't rest until I prove it."

** ** **

"Okay, Arthur, what you got for me?" Inspector Bishop cautiously entered the pathologist's domain, while being closely followed by Sergeant Tipping.

"Not much I'm afraid, Ben, she committed suicide, alright. Apart from her throat being slit, she had enough pills inside her to kill an elephant."

"Damn it, Arthur. I have just charged Dwyer with her murder, and all I've got is circumstantial evidence."

"Sorry, Ben, but there it is. I can't alter my findings just to suit your case."

"Perhaps we are looking at this in the wrong way." Sergeant Tipping interrupted thoughtfully.

"What do you mean?"

"Well, Dwyer said that she had received a poison pen letter the morning she died."

"Yes, well if you believe that, you'll believe anything. We only have his word for that."

"That's what I mean. Let's just say, for argument's sake, that he's telling us the truth. Whoever sent that letter is guilty of her murder, sir. We should be looking for the letter's author."

"Then I'll just have to prove that Dwyer wrote it, won't I? I reckon it's time we talked to his brother, the priest. After all, he found her, and I want to know why he was at that house and why he had removed vital evidence from a crime scene. If he did that is. Come on, sergeant, we've got work to do."

"How's the toothache. Ben?" Arthur Fellows looked up while spraying the cold metal slab free from blood; as Ben Bishop turned to leave.

"Bloody awful, Arthur. Have you got anything to keep me going, until I can get the bloody thing pulled out?"

* * * *

Ellen Cooper stood before the façade of the huge Victorian building that housed every retired priest, in the diocese, who needed care. While looking up, she noticed a small bird, high in the sky, suddenly swoop down before landing in one of the building's crevices to feed its hungry young. "The circle of life," she whispered, while thinking of the building's decaying inhabitants who lived within the building's ancient walls.

"Yes, may I help you?" A trim young woman in a nurse's uniform opened the oak door which in itself reminded Ellen of a church.

"My name is Ellen Cooper and I have an appointment to see Father Michael at 2 pm."

"Please, come in. He is expecting you."

"Thank you."

She entered the scrupulously clean entrance hall which smelt strongly of polish, before smiling at the young nurse.

"Please, wait here. I'll see if he's ready to receive you."

"Certainly, thank you."

It wasn't long before she was being led towards a group of priests that were playing poker. All were jealously holding their cards closely up to their chests. All were resisting the devil's temptation to cheat.

"Father Michael, you have a visitor."

The old man, who had a youthful eye, looked up and smiled, before indicating to the group of priests that the game of poker had prematurely ended, and that they were to disperse.

"Let's make them all jealous. Come, sit beside me, my dear." He smiled while patting the now vacant chair. "Have you brought what I had asked for?"

"Yes, of course." Ellen withdrew out of her bag, a half bottle of whisky in a brown paper bag which he quickly placed under his cushion.

"Good, now let's have some tea." He raised his hand and the young nurse scurried away to do his bidding.

"Now, you said on the telephone, that you wanted to know about the Dwyer boys. I have read in the paper that Brian is in trouble with the police."

"That's right, Father. He's been charged with murder, and I believe that he's innocent."

"Why do you think that, if, as you say, you don't know him?"

"I couldn't tell you, it's just a gut instinct that I have. Father, please help me, if I am right, an innocent man will be sent to the gallows."

A tray of tea duly arrived and the old priest, once the coast was clear of course, tipped a little whisky into his cup. Leaning back, he closed his eyes as the burning liquid ran down his throat.

"That's better. Now what do you want to know?"

"Everything, I want to know everything that you know."

"Very well. I'd better start from the beginning then." He closed his eyes while sipping tentatively at the hot tea. "I was only a young priest when the Dwyer boys came in with their mother. She wanted me to accept them to be trained as servers."

"And did you accept them?"

"Yes, there wasn't any reason not to." He paused while in deep thought. "They were both religious boys, you know. They came from a religious family, their mother more so, yet John always worried me."

"Why?"

"He was too religious, too pious. Boys of his age should be getting up to mischief. I know Brian did, he was always chasing the girls, yet not John. John was the serious one. He never put a foot wrong."

"And that troubled you?"

"Yes, at the time, it worried me deeply. You see." He paused while taking another sip of tea. "John was always jealous of Brian. Did you know that he once set fire to his bedroom?"

"No, I certainly didn't know."

"Yes, his mother was frantic with worry. I advised her to send Brian away for a while, just to see whether it would break John's behaviour. Give the situation time to cool down, I thought. She agreed, and she sent him off to his grandmother's somewhere on the coast, I believe, I don't know where."

"Did it help?"

"I believe it did for a while, yet it all started up again."

"How, what happened?"

The old priest paused, looked about himself, and poured another cup of tea with a liberal helping of whisky before replying.

"He tried to kill him. Almost pulled it off too. If it wasn't for his mother, he would have. Jealousy, my dear, it's a terrible thing, you know."

"How did he try to kill him?"

"He attacked him with a knife. Eventually John was sent to boarding school where he studied theology, and eventually trained for the priesthood. Yet even then there was trouble. Did you know Brian was once engaged?"

"No, I didn't know."

"Well, he was. Nice girl. Everything seemed to be going well for Brian, until she received a poison pen letter. Apparently this letter said some terrible things about Brian. All lies, of course, yet she believed it, and the relationship was ruined. The engagement was eventually called off. It broke Brian's heart, of course. It was a terribly sad time for everyone. Mind you, I'm not saying that John sent it, it could have been anybody, yet I had my suspicions at the time." The old priest replaced his cup onto the tray with a shaking hand. "There you are, my dear, now you know all that I know."

"Thank you, you've been most frank." Ellen slowly began to rise from her chair. "I'm grateful to you, and for all your help."

Suddenly his hand gripped hers, bringing her back down onto her seat.

"Be careful, my dear." Looking into her eyes, his voice held a cautionary tone. "Remember what I have told you. Jealousy is an evil thing; it takes you over and strangles all reasoning."

"I will, I promise you, thank you once again for your help."

Chapter Seven

Father Dwyer checked the morning's readings from the large open book that was sitting on the lectern, which stood by the side of the long altar. Turning the pages over until he had reached the day's correct reading, he paused for a brief moment before marking the page. Feeling an unease which he just couldn't shake off, he sighed. The police had come to see him the previous evening at the vicarage. He had fervently denied seeing any letter by Valerie's body. Neither was there any suicide note. Why would there be? Valerie found it exceptionally difficult to write because of her nervous condition. He had stated that his brother must have been confused about his finding a letter. After all, Brian had only just lost his wife, and was under terrible emotional stress. He must have been confused, which was totally understandable given the circumstances. As for being at the house, well he has been naturally concerned about Valerie for some time now, and on passing, he decided to call in to see her. It was all just a terrible coincidence that he was visiting on that particular awful morning. Yet he had been pleased that he had done so, as if he hadn't, Brian would have discovered her upon his return, which would have been far more traumatic for him. The police had seemed satisfied by his reasoning when they eventually left. After all, he is a priest, and priests don't lie, do they?

"You're bound to be worried, John, with him being charged with murder." He could now hear his sister Mary speak self-righteously while cooking their breakfast. "I don't know why you bother with him, even when we were kids, he was always in trouble. His being charged with murder wouldn't affect your standing in the community, would it? I mean the Bishop doesn't need to know, does he?"

"The Bishop," he subconsciously muttered, while descending the altar steps. "I must notify the Bishop."

Hurrying down the corridor towards the vestry, where the only working telephone was situated, he literally banged into Mrs Jenkins who was walking in the opposite direction.

"Why, 'ello Father. Yu seem to be in a 'urry this morning."

"Oh hello, Mrs Jenkins, I'm so sorry." Father Dwyer flushed and immediately stepped aside. "I didn't see you, please forgive me."

"Not at all, Father, not at all. Is there anything that I can 'elp yu with, Father?"

"No, no, thank you, Mrs Jenkins. I'm just on my way to the vestry to use the telephone."

"If it's still working, that is, Father. Last week it packed up completely so it did. The telephone people took days to fix it." She threw her plump hands up in the air with an exaggerated flair. "Oh, these terrible air raids. They frighten me, so they do."

"Yes, yes…I know what you mean, Mrs Jenkins. Man's inhumanity to man as they say." He began to scurry down the corridor, when Mrs Jenkins suddenly called out after him.

"By the way Father…did your lady guest find out what she wanted to know from Father Michael?"

"Pardon me?" Mrs Jenkins simple question caused Father Dwyer to turn sharply upon his heels to face her. "What did you say? You spoke to Mrs Cooper?"

"Aye, I did, Father." She slowly walked towards him, and standing in front of him, she now felt strangely fearful. "She came 'ere last week asking questions, so she did."

"She came here? What did she want to know?"

"Nothing much, Father, she was only asking about your brother, Brian."

"What did she want to know about him, tell me?"

"As I say, nothing much, Father."

"What did you tell her?"

"Nothing, Father, I only said that I wasn't going to gossip, and I directed her to see Father Michael at the retirement home, as he had trained you both to be servers when you were kids…that was all."

"You should have directed her to me, Mrs Jenkins."

"I'm sorry, Father, if I've done anything wrong."

"No, it's alright, Mrs Jenkins, the harm's done now. In future, if anyone asks you questions concerning my brother, or myself for that matter, you are to direct them to me. Do you understand?"

"Aye, Father. Of course, Father. I'm sorry."

"No, no, it's perfectly alright. You weren't to know. Thank you for telling me though, Mrs Jenkins. Good day to you."

"Good day to yu, Father."

* * * *

The atmosphere in the vicarage dining room was heavy and subdued, as the three occupants ate their evening meal. Ellen inhaled deeply, while smiling in Mary's direction.

"The weather has been nice today, hasn't it?" Desperately she tried to make small talk yet to no avail. "I thought that I would go out to the shops tomorrow, if there's any shops still standing that is?"

"There should be. If you have any spare coupons, I would be grateful if you could use them on provisions, as we are running rather low."

"Yes, of course I will. I didn't think, I'm sorry Mary. Would you like to come with me? We can pool our coupons and have a girl's outing." She laughed, yet her laugh sounded false.

"I haven't got any coupons to pool, my dear." Mary's voice held an uncharacteristically worried tone. "Least ways, not until next week."

"I'm sorry, Mary. I'll bring in what I can."

"Thank you, dear."

"I banged into Mrs Jenkins this morning." John Dwyer looked up and fixed Ellen with a cold stare.

"Oh, did you? How is she?"

"Fine as far as I know. She told me that you had been asking questions about Brian and she directed you to see Father Michael. Is that true?"

"Yes, it is true. You sound as if there's a problem, is there?"

"No, not at all. I was only wondering why you went to see Mrs Jenkins. After all, if you wanted to know anything about this family, you only have to ask either Mary or myself."

"I just happen to be passing the church, I felt cold, and so I went in. Mrs Jenkins kindly asked me if I needed anything, and I asked her about Brian. I'm sorry if I've upset you, but there's really no secret about it."

"Well, did you go and see Father Michael?"

"Yes, yes, I did."

"What did he tell you?"

"Nothing really, we just talked about old times, when you were boys training to be servers. I believe he enjoyed reminiscing really."

"And that's all?"

"Yes, that's all."

A heavy silence engulfed the room which was only broken by Mary, who suddenly rose from her chair, and began to gather the empty plates.

"Well, does anyone want any pudding? There isn't much left over from yesterday yet I can stretch it to three if we all want a piece."

"No, thank you, Mary." Ellen rose slowly from her chair. "I have eaten quite enough, thank you. I think, if you don't mind, I'll take a little night air before I turn in."

"Of course, dear, don't go too far now; there may be an air raid."

"Thank you, Mary. No, no I won't go far, I promise. If the siren sounds, I'll come straight back."

"Okay, mind how you go, dear."

On hearing the door quietly closing behind Ellen Cooper, Father Dwyer glanced towards his sister and smiled. "Don't worry about me either, Mary, I think I'll go into the study to work on the church's accounts."

"Are you sure, John?"

"Yes, thank you, the accounts are overdue as I've been lazy. I really must get them done now otherwise I'll miss the deadline. Don't disturb me, Mary. I'll see to myself."

"Okay, John, if you're sure."

Chapter Eight

"Bishop!"

The booming voice of Chief Superintendent Morgan echoed down the corridor, causing Ben Bishop to quickly throw his half-eaten sandwich in the top draw of his desk while frantically picking up his pen and pretend to write.

"Yes, sir, how lovely it is to see you, sir."

"Cut the crap." Glancing towards Sergeant Tipping, he indicated for him to leave. "Go and get yourself a coffee, sergeant."

"Yes, sir."

"What the bloody hell are you playing at, Bishop?"

"I don't know what you mean, sir."

"You know perfectly well what I mean, Bishop. I have Dwyer's representatives crawling all over me, and you're here, eating a bloody sandwich. Brilliant!"

"Oh, come on, sir." Ben Bishop rose from his chair and standing by the crime chart, began to stab his finger at the two prostitute's photographs, his voice rising with emotion. "These are the two women that Dwyer was having sex with on a regular basis, they are now, both dead. He also had sex with countless of other prostitutes that we don't even know about. They're probably dead too and just listed as missing. His first wife, who just happened to be insured up to her neck, died under suspicious circumstances, and now his second wife, who is also insured up to her neck, is dead. By her own hand admittedly, but I bet he drove her to it."

"You have proof of that, do you? I mean hard proof."

"No, I know it's just circumstantial, yet I am getting the proof, I just need time. Please, sir."

"No, Ben, you're out of time. I want Dwyer released, and released now."

"But you can't do that, sir. You know as well as I do, you get a gut instinct doing this job. I just know this man did it, and I would much rather have him jumping up and down in a police cell than to be out there somewhere, sticking a knife into another woman."

"I want him released, Bishop."

"Please, don't do this, sir. I'm getting the evidence. Just give me twenty-four hours."

"No. I want you to release him **now.** And if you don't, I will."

Ben Bishop walked towards his boss. "Please, sir, just twenty-four hours, that's all I ask."

"Look, Ben, you're a bloody good copper, yet you of all people should know, you have to get a water tight case together before you can charge him. No, before you do that, you come and see me first, and ask me whether you have enough evidence to charge him with. Do I make myself clear, Bishop?"

"Yes, sir."

"Now, don't go back to eating. Get off your arse, and get out there, and find the man who did this, stop pratting about. **Do I make myself clear?**"

"Yes, sir."

"Don't muck this one up, Bishop."

"It wouldn't be the first time, sir."

"No, but it might be the bloody last." He briefly smiled; his shoulders dropped which caused his voice to soften. "Look, Ben, my bosses are after taking you off this case. I've held them back so far, yet I can't hold them back for much longer. What about this diary that you found in the victims flat? Did you get any leads from that?"

"No, not really, sir." Ben Bishop sighed. "Most of her contacts were soldiers out on the town for a good time. We checked them all out, yet most of them are either dead or missing. We do have a record of Dwyer though. Over a period of time, he's paid her a lot of money, no wonder his practice is struggling."

"It's not much to go on though, is it? Look Ben, go and do your job, get out there and find out who's doing this. In the meantime I'll do mine, and that's shielding your arse."

"Yes, sir, thank you, sir."

"Don't thank me, I want results and if I don't get them, and get them soon, your neck is on the block."

He left quietly, leaving a very subdued Ben Bishop looking at his office's closed door.

* * * *

Several hours had passed since Ben Bishop had been reprimanded by his superior, yet he still felt bruised. His toothache didn't make matters any better either, as it throbbed with even more severity, which caused him to rub his cheek while looking towards his sergeant who also seemed to be chastising him.

"Well, I told you, sir. I never did like the way we ignored the handbag being deliberately placed for us to find, with the doctor's name and address inside. It's all too convenient."

"I believe I told you that, sergeant, or had you forgotten?"

"No, sir, I hadn't forgotten, yet you ignored your own advice, didn't you?"

"Yes I did, because I thought we had our man. Tell me, who else could have killed these women? The prostitutes that we've interviewed all knew Dwyer, and the two women who were killed were having sex with him, everything points to him."

"I know that, sir, yet I think we're on the wrong track. I just don't think he did it."

"Bloody hell, what a mess."

Ben Bishop slowly shook his head while taking his raincoat down from the hook behind his office door. "I just feel that that bastard is the only one who has a motive. I can't see anyone else who would want them dead bad enough to murder them. Oh, come on, sergeant; let's find out who did this."

Inspector Bishop and Sergeant Tipping walked side by side down the wide steps of the police station to where their black Wolseley car awaited them.

"Sir, sir, come back, sir!" A police constable rushed down the stairs after them, waving in the air a sheet of foolscap paper.

"Yes, officer, what's the matter? Station on fire?"

"There's been a hit and run, sir."

"So what's that got to do with me?"

"The Chief has told me to give it to you, sir. He thinks it's linked to your case."

"Why? What's it got to do with Dwyer?"

"The victim was staying at the vicarage with Dwyer's brother, sir."

"Now, will you believe me?" Ben Bishop turned towards Sergeant Tipping. "I just knew I was bloody right."

"No, sir, it wasn't Brian Dwyer. His release was delayed because of a mix-up with his papers. No sir, he's still with us, he's still in the cells."

Chapter Nine

The evening was drawing ever nearer, when Ben Bishop, while rubbing his sore chin, led his sergeant through the hospital's front entrance in a thoughtful manner.

"What's the matter, sir, tooth still playing up?"

"Yea, bloody thing, the quack dentist is pulling it out tomorrow, for some exorbitant fee. I'd pull it out myself if I wasn't such a bloody coward."

They both glanced towards each other and smiled, while climbing the stone stairs which led towards the side room where Ellen Cooper laid.

"I'm Inspector Bishop, and this is my sergeant, Sergeant Tipping. We are here to see a Mrs Ellen Cooper. I believe she was admitted late this afternoon."

"Oh yes, we are expecting you." The slim young woman, who was clad in a clean, starched uniform, rose from the chair which was situated behind the reception desk. "If you care to follow me, inspector, I'll take you to see her."

Ben Bishop glanced towards his sergeant who was smiling.

"Keep your mind on the job, Tipping."

"Sorry, sir."

"You're supposed to be a married man, for Christ's sake."

"Well, just because the pubs are open all hours, it doesn't mean that you can't drink elsewhere, does it?"

"She's in here, inspector." The nurse turned, halting their conversation. "Please, don't be too long, she's due to be taken down to the theatre shortly."

"Are her injuries serious, nurse?"

"No, her main injuries are where the car impacted on her legs, inspector. Otherwise she's been extremely lucky. Her left leg has been smashed, that's why they're operating, yet apart from that, it's mainly cuts and bruises. Remember, only five minutes."

"Yes, of course. Thank you, nurse."

Slowly and quietly the two men entered Ellen Cooper's dimly lit room. Sitting by the bed, Timothy Tipping extracted his police notebook from his coat pocket.

"Ellen, Ellen Cooper, can you hear me, Ellen?" Inspector Bishop whispered. "Can you hear me, Ellen? I'm a police officer, and I've come to find out who hurt you."

Slowly, very slowly, Ellen opened her eyes while wincing with pain.

"Ellen, can you tell me who hurt you, love? Did you see who did this to you?"

"No." she whispered in a croaked voice. "He came from behind."

"Is there anything that you can remember about the car? Perhaps its colour or make. Anything Ellen, I know you're in pain, love, but please try to remember something."

"Jealousy." She whispered.

"Jealousy? I don't understand, Ellen, you're losing me, love."

"Jealousy, the root of all evil...talk to Father Michael."

"Father Michael? Who is he, Ellen?

"Look to the church." Closing her eyes, she finally whispered. "That's where you will find the answer."

* * * *

One week had passed, which had seen Ben Bishop suffering a painful tooth extraction and a meeting with his superior officer. Chief Superintendent Morgan wanted results, and he wanted to know exactly why his inspector wasn't achieving them. They had eventually found Father Michael at the priest's retirement home. It had cost them a whole bottle of whisky to be able to speak with him, yet it was well worth it. Looking up at St Joseph's church, Ben Bishop felt physically and emotionally bruised as he stood beside his Sergeant Timothy Tipping.

"Well, sergeant. Ellen Cooper has taken us this far."

"Father Michael was very informative, don't you think? Especially once he had three cups of tea."

They both smiled. "More like three cups of whisky. She also told us to look at the church."

"Perhaps we should find the priest and ask permission to search it, sir. There's obviously something in there that we haven't yet found."

"Like the shoes you mean, we still haven't found them, have we?"

"No, we haven't, or the first victim's handbag, if she had one that is."

"All women have a handbag, sergeant, come on. We won't get results by standing here talking. Let's find the priest, Father Dwyer."

Ben Bishop felt uncomfortable as he walked through the high archway that led towards St Joseph's entrance. He didn't know whether it was the church's gloomy interior, or the bloodied Christ who seemed to be following his progress from the cross.

"I don't like this type of church, Tipping, it's enough to make God-fearing folk turn atheists. Come on, let's see whether we can find the priest."

"He ain't 'ere."

The sound of an unexpected voice caused Ben Bishop to spin around while looking up at the crucified Christ.

"I told yu, he ain't 'ere."

"Bloody hell, she frightened the crap out of me." Ben Bishop visibly relaxed upon realising that the voice came from a mortal being and not an immortal force.

"Sir, you're in church." Sergeant Tipping sternly whispered. "Show some respect, will you?"

Both men smiled while watching a short plump woman with a little wobbly hat perched on top of her greying hair, approach them.

"Where did she come from?" Sergeant Tipping whispered.

"I don't know, ask him up there, he's supposed to see everything, isn't he?" Inspector Bishop whispered while motioning towards the crucified Christ that still seemed to be watching his every move.

"I told yu, Father Dwyer ain't 'ere."

"We are the police, madam. I am Inspector Bishop and this is my sergeant, Sergeant Tipping."

Mrs Jenkins closely examined the two warrant cards that were held out before her, and sniffed.

"Am I supposed to be impressed?"

"You should be."

"Well, I ain't, and I don't take too kindly to anyone blaspheming in me church either, even if they are the cops."

Ben Bishop coughed embarrassingly while trying to regain his composure. "Could you please tell us where Father Dwyer is, madam?"

"No, no, I can't."

"No, you can't, or no, you won't?"

"No, I won't."

Mrs Jenkins held Ben Bishop's angry glare without flinching, which, deep down, he admired.

"May I ask your name, please, madam?"

"If it's any of your business, me name's Mrs Jenkins, Mrs Joan Jenkins."

"Well, Mrs Joan Jenkins, I am a police officer, and I am investigating a murder enquiry. A murder that I believe took place right here." He pointed down to the smooth stone slabs that formed the churches flooring, while unflinchingly holding her gaze. "So if you don't tell me where Father Dwyer is, this instant, I am going to charge you with obstructing the police with their enquiries." His voice rose as he stepped towards her. "Would you like me to do that, Mrs Joan Jenkins? Would you like me to charge you with obstruction?"

"No."

"Then I'll ask you again. Where is Father Dwyer?"

"If yu must know, 'e's at the vicarage. Now leave, before I throw yu both out, go on, get out the both of yu."

* * * *

Half an hour later, Inspector Bishop glanced towards his sergeant while pressing the front doorbell of the vicarage.

"This should be fun, sir?"

"Not half as much fun as Mrs Joan Jenkins."

"Yes, gentlemen, can I help you?" Mary Dwyer stood before them, with one hand on the door, the other on the hall wall; Ben Bishop realised that she had been warned of their impending visit and was subconsciously baring their way. Instinctively he now knew that he was finally on the right track as once again, Ellen Cooper's words drifted into his mind. "Look towards the church...the church."

"We are the police, madam. My name is Inspector Bishop and this is my sergeant, Sergeant Tipping. May we come in?"

"Yes, if you must."

"We wish to speak to Father John Dwyer, is he here?"

"Why do you want to speak to John? It's Brian who you want to talk to, isn't it? He's the one who you charged with those murders?"

"As you are well aware, madam, we released your brother two days ago through lack of evidence." He paused while watching the disappointment visibly spread across her features. "Can you take us to see Father Dwyer, please, madam?"

"Very well, if you must, you'd better come this way."

* * * *

"John, dear, it's the police; they wish to speak with you."

"It's rather late for you to be playing house calls, isn't it, gentlemen?" John Dwyer looked up from a pile of papers, his voice mirroring his annoyance.

"We haven't got a nine-to-five job, sir."

"Obviously not. I thought that I had answered all your questions before, inspector, surely you haven't got much more to ask me."

"I'll be the judge of that, sir."

"Mary, can you please go and make us some tea or something?" John Dwyer ushered his sister out of the room.

"But why don't you want me to stay, John? I don't wish to leave. This is ridiculous; I have every right to stay."

"Please, Mary, we won't be long, I promise." Finally he closed the study door behind her, before turning towards the silent and ever watchful police officers.

"I'm sorry about that, inspector, how can I help you?"

"Where were you on the night Mrs Ellen Cooper was injured, sir?"

"Why do you want to know where I was? Surly you don't suspect me, inspector. I've known Ellen for years, she was my sister's old school friend."

"I'm sorry, sir, I have to ask."

"I was in here, of course, doing the accounts."

"Is there anyone who could vouch for your whereabouts, sir?"

"Of course, there is, my sister was here. This is ridiculous, utterly ridiculous."

Ben Bishop glanced towards his sergeant while slowly walking towards a small curtained window.

"Can you tell us where this window leads out to, sir?"

"The yard, of course, why?"

"And the yard, leads out to the car park, doesn't it?"

"I've had enough of this, inspector. If you insist on questioning me any further, I demand to speak to my solicitor."

"Now, why do you want to speak to your solicitor, sir? We are only enquiring of your whereabouts on the night Ellen Cooper was almost killed by a hit-and-run."

"This is intolerable, inspector."

"Your brother's daughter was killed by a hit-and-run, wasn't she, sir? They never did find the man who did it…did they?"

"No, they didn't. But what's that got to do with me?"

"Oh, we are just thinking out loud, sir…we spoke with a Father Michael a couple of days ago. Didn't we, sergeant?"

"We certainly did, sir."

"How did you know about him?"

"I think you know that, sir. I believe you knew Ellen Cooper had spoken to him and you were afraid that she would tell us what she knew, and that's why you tried to silence her."

"That's it, that's enough." Father Dwyer reached towards the telephone with his plump hand. "I'm phoning my solicitor. I am not answering anymore of your questions, until he's here."

"Oh that's a shame, sir, as I was just about to ask you about the affair you had with your brother's first wife. Is that why you drowned her? To keep her quiet: Did she try to blackmail you? She was turning the screws, wasn't she?"

The room fell momentarily silent as Father Dwyer slowly replaced the telephone back onto the receiver. Suddenly the study door opened and Mary Dwyer brought in a tray of tea. Placing it down onto her brother's desk, she began to pour out the tea pots contents.

"That's alright, Mary, we can manage, thank you." Almost pushing the protesting Mary out of the study, he closed the door quietly behind her.

"Yes, she was blackmailing me, inspector. She said that she would go to the bishop. She was going to tell him everything if I didn't give her money, and lots of it. I just couldn't give her any more, yet she wouldn't listen."

"So you drowned her."

"No, no, I didn't. It wasn't like that; it was just a terrible accident."

"A convenient accident for you though, wasn't it, sir?" Ben Bishop stepped towards the priest, who was now looking down at the floor. "And you have the gall to stand up in the pulpit, and preach to other people."

"We all live in sin, inspector."

"You call yourself a priest man, God's earthly representative, yet you have broken every vow that you have made to your God. You're nothing but a charlatan. You had an affair with your brother's wife."

"May God forgive me?"

"Your God might, yet I doubt whether your brother ever will." Ben Bishop paused while watching the priest's reaction. "Tell me, sir, when I last interviewed you, you stated that Valerie Dwyer didn't leave a suicide note."

"Yes, that's right, she didn't."

"You also stated that there wasn't any other letter near her body."

"That's what I said, yes."

"I don't believe you."

"Well, in that case, inspector, it's up to you to prove that I'm lying. Isn't it? Can you prove that I'm lying? Well, can you?"

Ben Bishop gave no reply.

"I thought not. Well, inspector, until you can, Valerie Dwyer died without a suicide note or any other note for that matter, near or around her body."

"I want the keys to the church."

Father Dwyer looked shocked. "Why, why do you want the keys to the church?"

Ben Bishop stepped towards the priest, their faces almost touching, as he slowly and quietly repeated. "I want the keys to the church now, please, sir, because I am going to search it from top to bottom, slowly and methodically. And if I find anything, anything that ties you into those murders...I'll be back, and I won't be having tea. Do we understand each other?"

"I have nothing to fear, inspector...you won't find anything; I can quite assure you of that."

* * * *

Inspector Bishop and Sergeant Tipping walked quietly out of the vicarage and down the three large stone steps that led down to the walkway, where their black Wolseley was parked.

"You were sailing close to the wind there, sir." Timothy Tipping glanced towards Ben Bishop and frowned, which was his custom when disagreeing with his boss's methods of interrogation. "You didn't know that he had an affair with Dwyer's wife?"

"No, I didn't, but the gamble paid off, didn't it?"

"What made you think that he had an affair with her anyway?"

"It's what Ellen Cooper said to us at the hospital, remember...'jealousy and church'. John Dwyer has been jealous of his brother since they were children. Father Michael told us that much. Anything and everything that made his brother happy, he either took away or destroyed. I wouldn't even put it past him if he hadn't had an affair with the second Mrs Dwyer either, before she became ill that is."

"You don't know that, sir."

"No, I don't, but I could have a bloody good guess. Come on, sergeant. We have to get proof this time. I have to nail that bastard before I can charge him."

"It's getting late, sir, I promised my wife that I would be home on the dot tonight as she wants to visit her mother, and it's my turn to look after the kids."

"If you kept your mind on the job, sergeant, perhaps we can all get home, on the dot."

"Yes, sir. We'd better go straight to the church, before he has a chance to warn Mrs Jenkins that we're on our way."

"She already knows, didn't you notice? Mary Dwyer was talking to her on the phone as we left."

* * * *

Mrs Jenkins did indeed know that her domain was about to come under siege by unscrupulous forces. *Forces of the nosey type: that will pry into Father Dwyer's affairs. Making a mess and turning everything upside down. Intolerable!* Putting anything of importance into locked draws and secret hiding places, she purposefully locked the vestry door and hid the key down her ample bosom.

"They won't get in there in a hurry."

Quickly running out of the church, she now made her way, as fast as her short legs would carry her, down to the crypt's entrance where ancient bones laid in ancient family vaults. It was dark, damp and gloomy which she had become accustomed to in her time working for Father John Dwyer. After all, he would be totally lost without her help in clearing up the odd mishap. She had always secretly loved John Dwyer. That was the reason why she had volunteered to become a church helper, just to be near him. For many years, she had helped and shielded him from any outside influences, influences which may or may not harm him. He never knew of her love, he only knew that she could always be relied upon when he had a problem to clear up. She now smiled at the very thought of him as she pushed an old wheelbarrow into one of the darkest of corners. No, they'll not find anything; she'll make damn sure of that.

Upon hearing a car driving up the gravel pathway towards the church, she ceased her activity. It's time for her to leave, to lock the heavy oak door of the crypt. It's time for her to watch and obstruct the disruptive forces that are now threatening to overpower her beloved priest.

"Where shall we start, sir?" Sergeant Tipping enquired while alighting out of the car.

"I think we should start at the top and work our way down, don't you, sergeant?"

"I don't think we will find much in the belfry."

"We might, on the roof, sergeant." Ben Bishop strode purposefully towards the churches entrance. "Come on, we've got some climbing to do."

Mrs Jenkins scurried around the back entrance of the church and, upon entering, quickly locked the door which sealed the staircase's entrance. Just before Ben Bishop's appearance. Breathing heavily, she flattened herself up against the darkened corner while listening intensely to Ben Bishop's frustration.

"Bloody hell, the damn thing's locked. Have you got the keys, sergeant?"

"Yes, sir."

Waiting with bated breath, she listened intensely to their efforts in opening the door. *They have the keys*, she thought to herself, *Why on earth did John give them the keys? Damn it.*

"That's the one, sir."

She listened, helplessly, to the lock sliding back, and the old iron hinges groaning as the heavy oak door was slowly pulled open. She was helpless, yet not beaten, not yet anyway. Following them up the stone steps and at a safe distance for them not to notice her, she now listened with some amusement to their futile efforts of deduction.

"There's nothing here, sir." She heard the sergeant's voice which held a puzzled tone. "This is a waste of time."

"I'll be the judge of that, sergeant."

Laughing quietly to herself, she turned to descend the stone staircase, when she heard the sound that she didn't think that she would ever, in her whole life, welcome.

"Bloody hell, it's the air raid siren, sir."

"I know that, sergeant, I've heard it often enough."

"Well, don't you think we had better start getting back? I need to see that my wife and kids are safe, sir."

"Yes, alright. It's getting late anyway, sergeant. We'll come back first thing the morning when there should be someone around." Ben Bishop glanced towards his sergeant who was about to exit the belfry. "Meet me in the office at eight tomorrow morning. I want to catch them by surprise."

Chapter Ten

The night had been long and sleepless, yet the morning's sun shone on Inspector Bishop and Sergeant Tipping as they stood bleary eyed in front of St Joseph's church.

"You look awful, sergeant."

"I feel awful, sir. Never mind, at least we're still alive."

"Yea, at least we can be thankful for that. Come on, let's start searching."

Father Dwyer, who was standing in the entrance of the church, watched with trepidation as the two men approached. "Good morning, gentlemen, I see you are back again." He smiled yet his eyes reminded Timothy Tipping of a dead fish that was laid out on the fishmonger's marble slab.

"Yes, sir, we are." Ben Bishop noticed the priest's cassock that was scrupulously clean and starched with fine lace running round its circumference. "Is there a service being held today, sir?"

"Yes, the church is always open for His flock, inspector. No matter what Hitler throws our way."

"That's the spirit, sir, never bow to tyranny."

"Exactly, inspector: The spirit of the Lord is always with us."

"Well I hope you're right, sir. In the meantime, Sergeant Tipping and I have some work to do."

"I do hope that you will be circumspect when conducting your enquiries, inspector, I do not wish my service to be interrupted."

"Certainly not, sir, we will be very circumspect and very thorough. Won't we, sergeant?"

"Oh indeed, sir: very thorough."

Father Dwyer's smile faded, yet his cold eyes never left theirs as he stepped aside to allow them to pass.

"Come on, sergeant, this place gives me the creeps. Let's start with the vestry."

* * * *

"Something isn't right here."

"What do you mean, sir?"

"Well think, the priest is robed and ready to take the service, yet the vestry door is locked."

"Well, perhaps he locked it. He may be holier than thou, sir, yet even he doesn't trust the thieving buggers around here."

"Perhaps. Have you got the keys that he gave us last night?"

"Yes, sir."

It wasn't long before they were searching through the pockets of every cassock that were housed in an old wooden wardrobe, yet every drawer was locked to them, every cabinet, and even the safe was locked against their inspection, which caused Inspector Bishop to angrily growl.

"Get that bloody priest in here. I want these drawers open."

"You can't, sir, not now, the service has started."

"Bloody hell!"

"Sir, mind your language, we're in church."

Taking no notice of his sergeant's indignation, Ben Bishop started towards the door. "Come on, sergeant, I've had enough of this place. Let's get some fresh air and wait until that pious bastard has finished his sermon."

Little did they know that every move that they had made and every word that they had uttered had been observed by Mrs Jenkins, who had become more and more incensed by their disrespect of the sacred church and of its hardworking priest. Determined to halt their intrusion into Father Dwyer's secret affairs, she now shadowed their every move, unseen and unheard, as they made their way out of the church.

"You know there's one place that we haven't even thought of searching." Timothy Tipping glanced towards his boss, while pointing to the side of the church.

"Where's that?"

"The crypt; I reckon that's a good a place as any to hide something that you don't want to be found. Don't you?"

"Yes, I do, good thinking, sergeant. Come on, let's see if it's locked."

It was indeed locked, as every other door had been locked before it, stopping their progress, or at the very least, severely delaying them. Finally, after trying several keys, the crypt door slowly opened with a squeak revealing a pitch black void.

"Can you see a light switch anywhere?"

"Yea, I think this may be it, sir. Bloody hell!"

Suddenly Sergeant Tipping lost his footing and tumbled down several stone steps that led down to the crypt.

"You alright down there, sergeant? You haven't broken your neck or anything, have you?"

"No, sir, I'm okay."

"Thank God for that. I thought at first I would have to call Arthur in. Mind you, you wouldn't need a funeral, would you? I'd just stick you in one of those coffins."

"Thanks sir, I'm sure the wife would be grateful."

With the crypt only half lit, Inspector Bishop carefully made his way down the slippery stone steps, towards his stricken sergeant, and together they looked about themselves; seeing the ancient coffins that were coated in dust and cob webs, they shivered.

"God, it stinks down here. Come on, there's nothing here. Let's go."

They quickly made their way towards the entrance when Ben Bishop abruptly stopped. Turning towards his sergeant, who looked a pale hue in the half-light, he motioned back towards the ancient coffins.

"Were you afraid as I was back there?"

"Yes, sir, I was scared shitless."

"Yes, and who wouldn't be? No one likes coffins, do they? Come on, sergeant, if he's hidden those shoes anywhere, it'll be here."

* * * *

Pure fear gripped Mrs Jenkins as she listened to Ben Bishop and his sergeant searching the crypt. What was she to do? Father Dwyer was still conducting the service so she couldn't warn him. Or could she? Her mind was racing as to how she could prevent her way of life, and more importantly, Father Dwyer's life, from falling apart.

Suddenly, all was clear, there was only one way out and it was up to her and only her, to save the day. Quickly running back to the church, which caused her little hat to wobble alarmingly, she raced back to the vestry to retrieve the only weapon to hand, her gun.

* * * *

"You don't want me to look inside the coffins, do you, sir?"

"No, I don't think even my stomach is up to that task, sergeant. Just concentrate on the dust, has any dust or cobwebs been disturbed on or around them?"

"Thank God for that. There's some that have been broken into."

"Leave those, he wouldn't hide anything in them, just concentrate on any complete coffin that's been disturbed."

Walking slowly, they progressed side by side down towards the back of the crypt, where only living insects were company for the ancient dry bones.

"Sir, I really don't like this. This is spooking the shit out of me."

"I know, me too Tim, just keep looking. It's only the living that hurt you, not the dead."

"You called me Tim, sir."

"Shut up, and keep looking."

Slowly and methodically, they continued to look on and around the coffins until they found themselves at the very back of the crypt.

"What the hell?" Sergeant Tipping peered through the darkness into the back corner of the crypt. "What's this doing here? It's an old wheelbarrow sir. This isn't the place where you keep a wheelbarrow."

"It is if you want to hide it, that's how he transported the bodies. He wheeled them through the bloody streets in a wheelbarrow. Come on, sergeant, keep looking, those shoes have to be here somewhere."

So they kept searching, they searched behind and around the coffins with their bare hands, yet their efforts were fruitless: they now felt damp, filthy and smelled even worse. Suddenly Ben Bishop paused.

"Wait a minute, let's just think. If you wanted to hide something and you didn't want it to be found, where would you hide it? Think, man."

Timothy Tipping scratched the top of his head in thought, before suddenly exclaiming. "In the darkest, dustiest and filthiest place that I could find, sir."

"Exactly, so nobody would ever want to go near it, just like us. It has to be a broken coffin, sergeant. He's hid them inside a broken coffin!"

* * * *

Mrs Jenkins felt strangely calm as she silently watched the two police officers making their way towards the plan brown coffin, which had lain for years, broken, upon the stone shelf. Its occupant had long been forgotten, and the shroud had long been eaten by moths and other creatures that feed upon the dead. Only the bones now remain as evidence of a life that had once existed. In her mind, she had given the lifeless bones a reason for existing, a purpose that they wouldn't otherwise have had. Namely, to hide the evidence of Brian Dwyer's loose morals, that so shamed and appalled Father John Dwyer and threatened to bring down a good man's reputation. A reputation that she and she alone had to protect at all cost.

"I've found them, sir, I've found them, they're in here!"

"My God, we've got the bastard."

Mrs Jenkins gripped the gun with a slippery hand; it's now time, it's now time to protect the only love which she had ever had in her empty life.

"That's far enough; ya ain't got no right to be down 'ere."

"We have every right, madam." Ben Bishop stepped in front of his sergeant, who was standing open mouthed in shock. "We are conducting a murder enquiry, a murder enquiry in which I believe you are part of, aren't you? You know what happened here."

"They were jezebels, one even came to confession to confess her sins after she had been with that man, she took communion which is an affront to God when you have such evil in your heart."

"What evil, to have sex with a man?"

"To have illicit sex, 'e's a married man."

"You mean Brian Dwyer."

"Yea of course, who do you think I mean."

"How do you know she had sex with him? The confessional is confidential, you couldn't know what she confessed to, not unless the priest broke his vows and told you."

"'E would never do that, 'e's a good man is Father Dwyer."

"Then how do you know, tell me, how do you know what she said in the confessional if you weren't told?"

"I followed 'er, I watched them together, it disgusted me."

"So you told Father Dwyer, didn't you? You told him who to kill."

"Yea, I wanted to protect 'im, to protect 'im from is sinful brother. 'E was dragging the Father's good name down with is debauchery so 'e was."

"So the priest murdered them, and then you disposed of their bodies late at night. Did you clean the blood up as well? Well, did you? Because there must have been a lot of it."

"I had to 'elp 'im, I 'ad to protect 'im."

"From what? What do you have to protect him from…himself?"

"No, 'is brother, 'is brother's evil, so 'e is. 'E's everything that John isn't. 'E 'ad to be stopped, I 'ad to stop 'im."

"So you tried to use us to get rid of him, didn't you?" Ben Bishop stepped further towards her. "You tried to send him to the gallows, to get him out of the way."

"Yea, but you're so stupid, stupid, yu let him go, didn't yu? Yu let 'im go free, you're so stupid."

"I let him go free because he's an innocent man, a man that you tried to murder; just to protect the true killer that you just happen to be in love with. Good God woman; and you call him evil."

"Yu ain't taking Father Dwyer away from me, I won't let yu, I'll kill yu first."

"No, please." Timothy Tipping interceded. "I'm a married man with kids, for God's sake woman, please."

"Turn around." Joan Jenkins pulled the trigger back and pointed the gun towards them. "Go on, face the wall."

"No!" Ben Bishop shouted while quickly stepping further towards her. "If you're going to kill us, you're going to have to do it while looking at us."

"Very well, have it yu own way."

"Joan Jenkins…put that gun down this instant!"

Mrs Jenkins spun around to be faced with Ellen Cooper, who was leaning heavily on her walking stick a few feet behind her.

"I said put that gun down, this instant!"

"Mrs Cooper, she's going to kill us!" Sergeant Tipping shouted while standing beside Ben Bishop who was holding him back by his arm.

"No, you're not going to kill anyone, are you, Joan? You wouldn't do that, would you?"

"They know, they will take Father Dwyer away from me, they're going to kill 'im."

"You're in love with him, aren't you, Joan? You love him."

"Yea, yea I love him alright; I've loved 'im for years so I 'ave."

"God is love, isn't he, Joan?"

"Yea, yea, God is love, alright. 'E would smile on me, so 'E would." Joan Jenkin's hand lowered slightly, while a brief smile touched her lips.

"NO! God could never approve of your love. Your love is a mortal sin, he could never forgive that, Joan, God is love and light, yet the evil in Father Dwyer is darkness. Your love is a sham."

"Yu bitch, nooooo!"

Ben Bishop saw his chance, and springing forward, threw himself onto the startled woman, knocking the gun out of her hand, and causing it to slide across the floor. Timothy Tipping frantically helped his boss to pin Mrs Jenkins hands behind her back before handcuffing her.

"Mrs Joan Jenkins." Ben Bishop's voice held a relieved tone. "You are under arrest on suspicion of conspiracy to murder, before and after the fact. I must caution you that you are not obliged to say anything, unless you wish to do so, and what you say will be put into writing and maybe given in evidence."

Ellen Cooper slowly walked forward and picking Mrs Jenkins little straw hat up from the crypts dirty floor, looked soberly towards the sobbing woman.

"Your little hat has finally fallen, Joan, just like you…It didn't survive after all."

* * * *

Father John Dwyer smiled at an elderly couple, as they exited from the church. "Thank you for attending, I hope to see you again next week." He reached out and shook their hands.

"Goodbye, Father, very nice service."

"Thank you, Mr Jarvis, I hope to see you both again next week."

"Yes, we will be here, Father, if the Hun doesn't get to us first."

"Yes, indeed."

"Goodbye, Father."

His broad smile slowly vanished as he watched the two approaching men. "You want to speak to me, gentlemen?"

"Father John Dwyer, you are under arrest on suspicion of murder. I must caution you that you are not obliged to say anything, unless you wish to do so, and what you say will be put into writing and maybe given in evidence. You must come with us now, sir."

"My clothes, inspector, I can't come with you dressed like this, may I change my clothes?"

"Yes, of course, sir. I will wait here for you."

"Thank you, inspector, that's very kind of you. I'll try not to be too long."

Timothy Tipping looked anxiously at the retreating figure of Father Dwyer as he hurried back into the dimly lit church. "Sir, do you think that's wise? He could escape out the back way."

"What, him? No, he's not the type, anyway where would he run to? Stay with him if you want, he's probably heading towards the vestry."

Sergeant Tipping left Inspector Bishop talking to Ellen Cooper, and following the priest into the church, he watched as Father Dwyer silently prayed in front of the altar. Moving closer, he momentarily lost sight of the priest as he hurried towards the vestry. Timothy Tipping felt an unease which engulfed him and he couldn't explain why. Hastily opening the vestry's door, he now knew, the room was empty, the priest had vanished.

"Inspector!" he shouted while running out of the church. **"Inspector!"**

"What's wrong?"

"He's vanished, sir, he's gone."

"Look out!" Ben Bishop shouted while scrambling out of the way with Ellen Cooper in his arms. With his white and black priestly robes flapping wildly in the air, Father John Dwyer silently fell from the roof of his own church. He resembled a fallen angel that had been expelled from heaven, before landing with a sickening thud onto the gravel path, just inches before them. Suddenly, a terrible high-pitched scream came from the police car, where Joan Jenkins helplessly witnessed her secret love fall to his death.

* * * *

The excruciating pain of grief engulfed Brian Dwyer to the point where he couldn't draw breath without pain. His heart was broken as he was told by Inspector Bishop that his brother had destroyed everything that he had ever held dear in his life. It was he who had sent so many poison pen letters to his wife, destroying her mental health, and then finally killing her. They also strongly suspected that he was also responsible for killing their daughter, as well as the other women that he had known or loved.

He had been walking for what seemed like hours through the bombed out streets of London, watching desperate and hungry people who brushed passed him, not knowing of his pain as they were too busy with their own survival to even notice him. He was pleased about that, for he didn't wish anyone to notice him; all he wanted to do was to disappear, to be invisible and to cry unseen and alone, for that is what he was now, wasn't he, he was totally alone.

He didn't make a conscious decision to walk to the vicarage, yet somehow he now found himself standing on the opposite side of the street while looking at the wooden plaque with his brother's name displayed on it in capital letters. The representative of God had almost sent him to the gallows, and had destroyed his life, yet he still loved his brother, he still forgave him, for he believed in the power of God more than His representative ever did. Suddenly the clouds parted and a ray of sunshine bathed him in its warmth, causing him to smile. Walking forward, he pressed the bell which rang throughout the house and waited. Slowly, very slowly, the black painted door opened to reveal Mary. She looked exhausted and her white tear-stained face creased in her effort to control her emotions as she looked down on her brother in surprise.

"Mary." Brian Dwyer whispered. "Can you ever forgive me?"

Momentarily pausing, she looked at the brother that she had rejected for so many years. How could she have been so wrong?

Falling into his arms, she sobbed. "Oh Brian…there's nothing to forgive…It is you that should be forgiving me. Please, Brian…please, forgive me, I'm so, so sorry."

Epilogue

Several weeks had now passed since that terrible day when Father Dwyer died by his own hand, several weeks in which Inspector Bishop had been credited for solving the Poison Pen case.

"Well done, inspector." Chief Superintendent Morgan warmly shook Ben Bishop's hand. "I knew you could do it. I had every faith in you."

"Thank you, sir, you're most kind."

Ben Bishop knew that those warm words were on the condition that he had succeeded. If he hadn't, well, the reception would have been very different. Both men smiled, yet both men knew that his reputation as an inspector is only as good as his last case. Secretly, he felt a fraud, as without Ellen Cooper's help in pointing him in the right direction, he was certain that the case would still be unsolved. That was why he had telephoned and asked to visit her at her home where she was still recuperating.

"Yes, of course, inspector. It would be lovely to see you, and please bring your nice sergeant with you."

So that was why, on a warm Sunday afternoon, Ben Bishop and Timothy Tipping were sitting on Ellen Cooper's small sofa with a glass of homemade elderberry wine.

"Would you care for a top up, inspector?"

"No, thank you, Mrs Cooper, I'm fine."

"Sergeant, would you care for more?"

"I wouldn't say no, Mrs Cooper, thank you, it's rather nice this, don't you think?" He glanced towards Ben Bishop who tried to smile. "What's it made of now? You did tell us, I'm sorry, Mrs Cooper."

"No, no, not at all, sergeant. I grow my own elderberries and I mix a little something in it, which is a trade secret of course."

"Of course."

Again they all smiled, before Ellen Cooper sitting down opposite Inspector Bishop, looked at him inquisitively.

"So you wanted to talk to me, inspector."

"Yes, I wanted to thank you for all your help. Without you, Mrs Cooper, we could have both been killed."

"Nonsense, she would never have pulled the trigger."

"What makes you say that?"

"She's a poor soul, inspector; she had weaved this imaginary world in her mind for so long, that she had come to believe it. She believed that she loved him and that she was protecting him from you or anything that threatened her fanciful world, yet she is not a murderer. No, sadly she left that side of things to him."

"Thank God you were there." Timothy Tipping took a mouthful of wine. "That's what I say."

"What made you look into the crypt, Mrs Cooper, why were you there at all?" Ben Bishop spoke in an inquisitive tone.

"Fate, inspector, pure and simple. I was visiting Mary, and she told me that you were searching the church. So when I arrived, I noticed that the crypt door had been left open, and I came over to investigate. As I said before, inspector, it was fate, pure and simple."

"Well, I can only thank you, you know; I would never have suspected him as the murderer."

"Why, because he was a priest? My dear inspector, you would be surprised at the evil which is carried out in the name of God."

"Everything pointed to the brother; I was so sure that he did it."

"You were so sure that you stopped looking. Tell me, what man murders his wife and then takes her shoes as a trophy, when he has a whole wardrobe full of them at home? He would have no need to take such a risk."

"Is that why you went to see Father Michael?"

She paused before drawing a deep breath. "Partly, I just couldn't shake off the feeling that the answer laid deep in the brother's past. What puzzles me is that Mrs Jenkins pointed me in Father Michael's direction. She didn't realise his importance, you see. Yet John Dwyer did, and that's why he tried to silence me. We were lucky, inspector."

"Lucky?"

"Oh yes, sergeant, very lucky. Without her pointing me in Father Michael's direction, we may never have known of John Dwyer's crimes, and an innocent man would have been sent to the gallows. Wouldn't he, Inspector?"

"Yes, I'm ashamed to say. I would have found the evidence to hang him in the end. I was just so certain that I had the right man."

"Yes…" She drew another long deep breath "…let that be a lesson."

"Tell me." Sergeant Tipping broke the heavy silence. "What happened to Mary the sister? Did she have to move out of the vicarage?"

"Oh yes, indeed, she had to make way for the next priest. Brian Dwyer's taken her in temporarily, until she can afford a little place somewhere for herself. Ironic, isn't it? The brother that she had blamed and hated for all these years has come to her rescue. At least some good has come out of all this heartache, poor woman."

"Yes, indeed, poor woman."

"I still don't understand why he did it though."

"Oh, you mean, the murders? Well, inspector, that's simple. Jealousy, an emotion as old as time itself; He just couldn't bear his brother to be happy in anything. Be it a toy that he destroyed as a child or be it a wife or lover that he destroyed as a man. He had to destroy everything that his brother held dear. It's as simple as that."

"Yet why then did he become a priest knowing that he had to take a vow of celibacy? He could have married and had a family of his own if he was jealous of his brother's life."

"You don't understand, inspector. No matter what path in life his brother had taken, he would have destroyed it. He didn't want his brother's life for himself: he literally didn't want his brother to have a life; he wanted him to suffer and that is why he killed those women, which is where the evil comes in. Now, do you understand?"

"I think I do, finally. Thanks to you, I think I do anyway."

"Nonsense, you would have got there in the end."

"How did he know?" Sergeant Tipping enquired thoughtfully. "I mean, how did John Dwyer know which prostitutes had been with his brother? Dwyer wouldn't have told his brother about them, would he?"

"No, the girls themselves told John Dwyer."

"Pardon? What do you mean they told Dwyer themselves?"

"Would you like some more wine, inspector?"

"No, no, thank you. What do you mean they told Dwyer themselves?"

"They are a group of God-fearing women, inspector; a small group of ladies who all attended the confessional before they started work, as did Brian Dywer. They are good women; they just haven't got anything else to sell, other than themselves. We all have to survive the best way we know how in these terrible times, inspector." She paused while looking at him with steel-blue eyes that pierced his moral conscience. "I even believe that one of them had taken communion, and that's when Mrs Jenkins followed her."

"That's right, sir." Timothy Tipping exclaimed excitedly. "Arthur told us that the first victim had eaten bread and wine before she died. He said it could have been communion bread."

"Exactly." Mrs Copper sipped her wine with a satisfied expression, while still holding Ben Bishop's gaze.

"How do you know all this?"

"What, that the women went to church before they started work? Oh, that's easy, inspector." She smiled at him which caused him to smile in return. "Their friends told me. There is quite a group of ladies who work the streets at various times in that area, inspector, and you would be surprised what we talked about when I befriended some of them. Of course, being the police, you would never get that close."

They all laughed, even Ben Bishop started to relax into the sofa's cushions while sipping yet another glass of elderberry wine.

"What do you think will happen to Mrs Jenkins, inspector?"

"She will stand trial, of course, for aiding and abetting before, and after the fact, and if she's found guilty, which she obviously will, she'll spend several years in prison."

"Not obviously, inspector, jurors are a fickle bunch. She's a simple woman, and her defence will play on that for all its worth."

"You just might be right there, who knows."

"Well, I know one thing." Timothy Tipping exclaimed. "This elderberry wine is really nice. You just have to tell us your secret ingredient, Mrs Cooper."

"Do I?"

"Yes, you do, come on, Mrs Cooper. You have to tell us before we leave."

"Very well, if you both insist, although you mustn't ask where I obtained it." She smiled while looking at them both in turn. "One quarter whisky; and three quarters wine; it's rather potent, I'm afraid."

"You can say that again." They all laughed, while holding out their glasses to be refilled. "Thank you, Mrs Cooper." Ben Bishop stated while raising his glass to toast his host. "Thank you for everything."